"Do I have to remind you that it was me you married, not him?"

"I want a divorce, Ben!" Nerissa broke out in a voice that shook, and the room filled with an intolerable tension.

"I'll fight it," he said curtly. "I'll use any weapon I have to—even if it means bringing *him* into it. What do you think that will do to your family pride?"

Dear Reader,

The Seven Deadly Sins are those sins which most of us
are in danger of committing every day: very ordinary
failings, very human weaknesses, but which can
sometimes cause pain to both ourselves and others.
Over the ages they have been defined as: Anger,
Covetousness, Envy, Greed, Lust, Pride and Sloth.

In this book I deal with the sin of Pride. In certain
circumstances, pride can be a strength and comfort,
but in other circumstances it can be deadly,
particularly when family pride leads people to lie, to
suppress the truth about the past, or when someone is
too proud to admit their feelings.

Charlotte Lamb

This is the first in Charlotte Lamb's new series, SINS.
Watch out in the coming months for six more
romances—all complete stories in themselves—where
this exceptionally talented writer proves that love can
conquer the deadliest of sins!

Coming next month: *Deadly Rivals*...the sin of
Covetousness. Have you ever hankered after
forbidden fruits?

Charlotte Lamb

Secret Obsession

Harlequin Books

TORONTO • NEW YORK • LONDON
AMSTERDAM • PARIS • SYDNEY • HAMBURG
STOCKHOLM • ATHENS • TOKYO • MILAN
MADRID • WARSAW • BUDAPEST • AUCKLAND

ISBN 0-373-11816-3

SECRET OBSESSION

First North American Publication 1996.

CHAPTER ONE

'I'LL be back on Friday week,' Ben said, his back to her but his reflection visible in the dressing-table mirror as his long fingers carefully knotted a blue silk tie, adjusted the set of his collar. Every movement was calm, unhurried, assured—as though he had all day to get ready.

It was Nerissa who was on edge, her blue eyes constantly glancing at the clock and away again quickly, before Ben noticed. He was too quick to pick up signals; he might start wondering why she was on tenterhooks to get him out of the house; he might ask questions and then she might panic and give away too much. That was what happened to a lot of people when Ben was interrogating them; she had watched it happen in court often enough— heard witnesses start stammering, go pale, flush, betray themselves.

From this angle she could see the razor-edge of his profile—intimidating, forceful, his mouth level, his grey eyes narrowed and intent. He smoothed down his tight-fitting waistcoat, checked the time by his watch.

Oh, God, why was he taking so long?

She took a deep breath to steady her voice, then said, 'Your taxi's waiting!' It had arrived early; the meter must be ticking away.

'I ordered it for eight o'clock and it is only just that now. He can wait,' he said in that deep, curt voice which made her tension worse.

If he didn't leave soon she was going to miss her train. In an agony of impatience she moved to the window, looked out through the lace curtain, saw the London street bathed in autumn sunlight, the horse-chestnut trees in the gardens opposite shedding their russet leaves in a brisk wind, having already shed the spiky orbs which split as they hit the ground, making it easier for the local boys to hunt among the leaves for the shiny brown nuts.

'It's going to be a beautiful day,' she said in melancholic irony. Wasn't that always the way? Weather always mocked you at times like this; it was never in the right mood.

It should be grey, elegiac, rain seeping down from dark clouds; the wind should howl across the city, or lightning strike the horse-chestnuts and set them blazing.

Instead, it was glorious out there—rich and glowing colours, a brilliant blue sky radiant with sunlight.

Ben clicked down the locks on his suitcase and lifted it to the floor. She hadn't even packed yet—she hadn't dared; it would have been too risky. She would throw a few things into a case while she waited for a taxi to come and collect her. She hadn't dared call one, of course. Nothing must alert Ben to the possibility that she was going away too.

'I'll ring you tonight, from The Hague,' he said.

She had her excuse ready, but her voice was slightly breathless, all the same. 'I may have to work late; Gregory wants me to go out to Worcester to see a client. We don't yet know the size of the job and it could take all day to assess. I don't know what time I'll get back.'

That much was true—Gregory had given her instructions for the job yesterday and she hadn't told him that she wouldn't be doing it. She would ring him later, before she left.

Ben's arms slid round her waist and he rested his chin on top of her head, on the cloudy dark mass of hair she hadn't yet brushed into order. She trembled as she felt his body touching her, his hands below her breasts, resting there lightly, the warmth of his blood reaching her through her jersey wool dress.

'Are you going alone? Or with Gregory? I don't trust Gregory an inch—I hope you don't let him flirt with you!' Ben was smiling as he said it, though. Her boss was a happily married man who had never shown the slightest interest in her. If Ben had even suspected that Gregory might fancy her his tone, his look would have been very different— and they both knew it.

'As if I would!' she said, trying to sound amused too, but so strung up that she couldn't quite manage it. He made her so tense.

They had only been married for three months. It had been a whirlwind romance; she was still breathless. It had happened too fast for her to be quite sure what she was doing. There was so much about him that she did not know.

Of course, marriage was always a gamble. Until you actually lived with someone you could never be quite sure about them, but that was doubly true about Ben.

She had met him a year earlier, at a party given
by one of his clients who happened to work with
her. Nerissa had hardly known anyone in the
crowded room and had backed into a corner with
a glass of white wine. The host had brought Ben
over and introduced them, then left again, and Ben
had asked her a series of questions about herself
to which he had got shy, monosyllabic replies.

She hadn't thought she would ever see him again,
but a few days later he had rung her at work and
asked if they could have dinner. A little uncertainly
she had accepted, and spent an evening with him
at a well-known restaurant in Mayfair. They had
talked—or rather, Ben had talked and she'd
listened. Ben had asked questions and she'd given
husky answers. Nerissa was not a talkative girl, but
that didn't seem to worry him.

Ben Havelock, she discovered, was a very successful and wealthy barrister. He had very little
spare time, so they hadn't seen much of each other
during those early months. Last spring, however,
he had managed to get a fortnight's holiday and
they had spent it together up in Northumberland,
where she had been born and had spent most of
her life.

That had been Ben's idea. He wanted to get
to know her better against her own background,
he said. He already knew that London was not
Nerissa's territory; she had a lost look at times—
she lacked the necessary skills for city life and
wasn't street-wise or sophisticated. Ben was a
Londoner, a city man, with all that that implied of
shrewd, hard-headed sophistication. Not much
surprised him, but Nerissa was different. She in-

trigued him; he wanted to find out what lay behind her façade, where she came from, what people had bred her.

He had achieved his aim. She hadn't wanted him to visit her home but he had insisted, and he had discovered a lot about her during those two weeks—more than she had meant him to know.

She had secrets she had wanted to keep; Ben had guessed at them within hours of their arrival. He worried her, disturbed her, but he had persuaded her to marry him all the same, in spite of her doubts and reservations.

'It will work,' he had promised her. 'All you have to do is forget the past. This is a new beginning. For both of us.'

He had memories he wanted to forget, too. He had told her about them freely enough, yet she still felt uneasily that she did not really know him very well. She had thought that once they were man and wife she would really know and understand him, but there was a darkness in Ben which still locked her out. She was beginning to be afraid it would always be there—a wall around him through which she could not pass and which hid a side of him which worried her.

The taxi hooted and she jumped. 'He's getting impatient!'

'Let him!' Ben turned her round and lowered his head. His mouth was possessive. She felt her pulses quicken, her body begin to burn. That was one side of their marriage which worked; they were passionate lovers. In bed she could forget her uncertainties—she might not yet have the key to Ben's mind, but his body was as familiar to her as her own.

Ben abruptly ended the kiss and, lifting his head, framed her face between his hands for a moment, staring at her as if trying to memorise the way she looked.

'Is there something on your mind?'

The curt question made her heart do a back-flip. She had known it would be hard to deceive him; his training in court made him too accustomed to reading expressions, picking up nuances.

'I'm not looking forward to being here alone, that's all,' she lied.

That was true enough and he knew it; she always felt uneasy about being in the house alone at night. London was a dangerous city, especially to a girl from a peaceful little village miles from anywhere.

He frowned but accepted the excuse. 'Why don't you ask one of the girls from work to stay with you while I'm away?'

'I might do that,' she murmured, knowing she wouldn't because she wasn't going to be here.

The taxi hooted again and Ben's mouth indented impatiently. 'I'd better go or I'll miss my plane! If I don't talk to you tonight I'll ring tomorrow.'

He kissed her again, quickly, then he was gone. She heard his feet on the stairs, the front door opening, slamming shut.

Leaning her face on the cold glass of the window, she watched him walk rapidly across the pavement and get into the back of the taxi. He leaned sideways to look out and up at her, his face briefly visible before the taxi vanished—a hard-boned, spare-fleshed face, cool grey eyes, a wide, controlled mouth, black hair springing from a window's peak on his high forehead.

He would be a bad enemy, she thought, and her nerves tightened. When he found out that she had lied, discovered where she had gone, she was going to find out just how dangerous an enemy Ben could be.

His hand lifted for a second; she waved back, then the taxi turned the corner and Nerissa hurried away from the window. She packed her case first, not caring what she folded into it—it wouldn't matter what she looked like so long as she took warm clothes with her; it would be cold up there.

Downstairs in the kitchen she left a note on the table for the girl who did their cleaning and had her own key to the house. Then she went into Ben's study, rang for another taxi, then switched on the answering machine to record phone calls, including those from Ben later, or any from his secretary, Helen Manners, a slim blonde woman in her late twenties who had made her dislike for Nerissa clear from the minute they had met.

As she leaned over the desk Nerissa's eye was caught by their wedding photo, half buried among a pile of law books.

They had been married on a summer morning— a civil ceremony with only a few guests—some family and a handful of friends. It hadn't felt like a real wedding, somehow; Nerissa had always believed that when she married it would be in her local village church, among the people with whom she had grown up. That brisk, businesslike exchange of vows in London had had no romance, no sense of joy. She had gone through it numbly, with a sense of disbelief.

Helen Manners had been there, very elegant in an olive-green silk dress, her blonde hair piled on her head in a French pleat and pinned there by a large bow made of the same material as her dress. She had long, shapely legs and displayed her tiny feet in handmade black high-heels; she had expensive tastes.

Nerissa didn't like her and it was mutual. Helen had raised one perfectly drawn black brow as she'd run her scornful eyes over Nerissa's plain, cream-coloured dress and the Victorian posy of summer flowers she carried in a silver holder.

Ben had seemed oblivious of his secretary's hostility to his new wife, just as he was indifferent to his sister's dislike of Nerissa. Ben's sister hadn't even come to the wedding, in fact. But then neither had any of Nerissa's family.

It had been an odd wedding.

Nerissa stared at Ben's face in the photo—tough and uncompromising, his eyes locked and hiding secrets.

Nerissa turned away, biting her lip. When he found out... She couldn't even bear to imagine what he would do to her. He was capable of killing; she was convinced of that. The dark vein in his nature ran deep, and his pride was stony, unbending. Any injury to that pride was never forgiven.

She shivered, which reminded her that she was going north—the weather at this time of the year would be cool if not downright chilly. She went back upstairs and found a warm, heather-coloured tweed coat, a purple woollen scarf and knitted gloves that matched—a Christmas present from Aunt Grace last year. Aunt Grace always made the presents she gave; she was very good with her hands, could sew and knit expertly. For much of Nerissa's life Aunt Grace had made most of her clothes on the sewing-machine in the little sewing-room looking out over the farm orchard.

Nerissa stiffened as she heard the unmistakable sound of a taxi throbbing away outside.

She ran downstairs and picked up her case, opened the front door and hurried out—a slightly built, almost fragile girl, with a wild cloud of dark hair around a pale, triangular face, dominated by those huge, cornflower-blue eyes.

'Where are we going, Snow White?' joked the taxi driver, turning to stare at her.

'King's Cross station, please.'

He started off, saying over his shoulder, 'Where are you off to, then, love?'

'Durham,' she said, hoping he wasn't going to talk to her all the way. She was in no mood for a light chat with a taxi driver. She had too much on her mind.

'Never been there—what's it like?'

Nerissa stared out of the window at London's busy, crowded streets and thought of the wind off the moors, the open sky, the dinosaur contours of the green and brown hills with their rounded shanks and bony shoulders lifting against the horizon.

She had missed it, ever since she'd left just over a year ago. She realised suddenly how much she ached to see it again.

'Cold, at this time of year,' she said. 'Durham is almost in Scotland, you know.'

'Don't fancy that much; give me lots of sun, that's what I need, especially in winter.' The taxi driver began to tell her about his holiday in Spain and how hot it had been there last month on the beaches of Torremolinos. Nerissa heard one word in every three.

She caught her train by the skin of her teeth. She had reserved a seat but her compartment was half-empty anyway, and got emptier as the journey continued up north. The train was an express and only stopped at a few stations—the important cities along this route. At intervals someone came round with a trolley containing sandwiches, crisps, drinks, but she wasn't hungry so she just had a coffee mid-morning. She spent the long journey staring out at the changing scene—the smoke-blackened chimneys of London, the grey and yellow London brick, the dull red tiles in the endless rows of little houses as they flashed through the suburbs, and then the flat, rather scrubby fields and hedgerows which succeeded them before they broke out into the real countryside of the heart of England.

By the time they were in the Midlands the sun was quite warm on the window, summer's last, flickering, expiring flame moving over the landscape, the autumnal trees, the stubbled fields, the mist-hazed hills in the distance.

She had not been north since the spring, since that visit with Ben, since her marriage.

Had she changed? she wondered, trying to remember how she had felt before she'd met Ben, how she had felt as she'd made that first journey southwards to work in London.

She grimaced, still staring out at the countryside flashing past. Of course she had. A lot had happened to her in London. She was very different from the girl who had left the farm all those months ago.

Would they notice? Did it show—was it visible? She bit her lip. Philip would see it; he knew her better than anyone else in the world. He would know at once that the Nerissa who had come back to them was not the same girl who had left the north a year ago to work in London.

Except that Philip might never get the chance to notice anything about her.

She flinched at that idea, her skin white, stretched, taut. Stop it! she told herself. Don't even think it. He is not going to die.

She looked at her watch; they were running to time. They would pull into York any minute, not much longer now. Her uncle would meet her at Durham. He would have the latest news.

As the train slowly steamed into Durham she collected her case and her other belongings and a moment later stepped down on to the platform, her long, slender legs admired by one of the porters hanging about waiting for someone to require his services.

'Carry your bag, miss?' he asked, but she shook her head.

'I can manage, thank you.' She hurried away with her case; it wasn't very heavy.

She saw her uncle before she reached him and waved, breaking into a run.

He hadn't changed, which was one comfort. Still tall and loose-limbed with iron-grey hair, a weathered countenance, deep-sunk pale eyes, John Thornton was a man who spent most of his days out in the open and it showed. Sun and wind had given him a skin like leather, the horizon-gazing eyes of a sailor and the slow patience of a ruminating animal—like those he looked after on his farm, the wiry upland sheep of the Northumberland hills.

'Nerissa—thank God you're here. We need a miracle.'

He bent and kissed her cheek, took her case from her. 'I was afraid your husband might not want you to come.'

'Ben's away, abroad.'

Their eyes met, exchanged wordless understanding. 'How long for?'

'A week,' she said, and saw her uncle's face tighten.

'A week? It's going to take longer than a week.'

She had realised as much, had known as she left her home that she was going for a long time. She hadn't been able to face telling Ben; she had known how he would react. His pride would never have agreed to letting her come. He would see it as a betrayal, a choice between him and Philip, and in a sense she supposed it was, but in another sense she had had no choice. She had had to come.

'How is he?'

'Bad.' The monosyllable was flat yet filled with pain.

Her eyes stung with unshed tears. As they walked out of the station Nerissa slipped her hand through her uncle's arm in a gesture of silent comfort.

He squeezed her hand against his side with an affectionate look, but didn't say anything. He was not a man who said much; he had spent so much time alone in the fields that he had almost lost the habit of speech. That was one reason why she had grown up saying so little, why she was disturbed by noise and busy city streets. Silence had been her environment for so many years.

'You'll want some food; they never have anything worth eating on the train these days,' he said as they drove away.

'I'm not hungry!'

'Nay, you must eat!' He shook his head at her, half smiled. 'Grace told me to make sure you did. Won't do any of us any good if you get ill too! We'll stop at a pub on the way, get a bite to eat there.'

They stopped at a pub just a stone's throw from the hospital, found a seat in a corner, then John Thornton went up to the bar to order them both a ploughman's platter—chunks of local cheese with pickles and salad and home-made bread.

'How's Aunt Grace bearing up?' Nerissa asked, sipping her glass of cider which had a strong, home-brewed taste of fermented apples, rich, golden, autumnal, sending a warm glow through her and making her feel slightly less strung up.

Her uncle looked sombre. 'She never leaves him. She's sat by his bed ever since it happened, talking to him. She's certain he'll hear her voice and start to wake up.'

A pang hit Nerissa. She bit her lip. 'How long is it now?'

'Since he went into coma? Three days. We thought...hoped...he'd come out of it sooner, but he hasn't, and the doctors can't tell us when he will...if he will.' His hands curled into helpless fists on the table between them.

'Of course he's going to get better! You mustn't think like that. It isn't like you to give up.' She gently uncurled his fingers, held them tightly. 'You know Aunt Grace won't stop talking until he wakes up in self-defence!'

He gave a reluctant chuckle. 'You bad girl, you! Lucky for you she can't hear you!'

Nerissa smiled at him. 'Have you finished your drink? Shall we go?'

If only took a few minutes to reach the hospital. She had spent a few days there once, years ago, when she'd had her tonsils out. The smell of polish and disinfectant and soap was familiar; her nostrils wrinkled at it. Their footsteps echoed on the stone floors as they tramped for what seemed hours along cream-painted corridors, up stairs, along more corridors, until they reached the intensive care unit where Philip Thornton lay, on a life-support system.

His mother sat beside the bed watching him unwearyingly and for a few seconds Nerissa and her uncle stood in the doorway, watching her while she was unaware of them, so intent on her son that she had no attention to spare for anything else.

Nerissa looked at him, too—and away again, appalled by what she saw. Everything his father had told her was suddenly a reality, in front of her; she hadn't believed it fully until that moment—now she had to.

It was a relief to look at her aunt instead. Grace Thornton was the opposite of her husband. Where he was tall, she was short; where he was thin, she was plump. His skin was brown and weather-beaten; hers was as soft as a rose-petal and as rosy as an apple.

His eyes were very pale blue and deep-sunk; hers were slightly protuberant, very bright and a warm, rich brown, and her curly, goldy-brown hair showed no trace of the grey which had taken over in his hair.

Her voice was soft and warm; it flowed unceasingly while Nerissa and John Thornton listened. She had always done all the talking in the family while her husband and her son and Nerissa listened, and it was somehow reassuring to hear her talking now—it made the alien hospital surroundings seem more homely.

'And the top field will be given a dressing this next week—if your father gets round to it—now the ploughing's done. The turnips are coming on nice, then when the sheep have eaten all the grass we can turn them into the top field to eat turnip tops—and turnips too, if need be. Did I tell you the vet had been to see that ewe we thought might be carrying? Well, she wasn't. Hardly worth keeping her; she hasn't lambed for eighteen months. Past it, I reckon. She can go to market with the others next time.'

John Thornton moved forward and his wife stopped talking and turned her head. She saw Nerissa and her face lit up.

'Here's your father now, Philip,' she said conversationally. 'And Nerissa's with him! There, I told
you she'd come, didn't I? And she looks just the
same; she hasn't changed.'

She got up and held out her arms; Nerissa ran
into them and they hugged, kissing. Aunt Grace
moved back to look at her, tears sparkling in her
bright brown eyes.

'You look well. She looks well, Philip. Lost
weight, mind. Skinnier than ever! Don't you eat
down there in London? Did your uncle take you to
have a bite to eat before you came here? I told him
to make sure you got some lunch first—I know
those trains—nothing but sandwiches and crisps;
that's all you get on them these days. In the old
days they had a proper buffet car and a three-course
lunch, with waiters in white coats and silver cutlery
and good glasses on the table, but these days they
can't be bothered.'

'We stopped and had a ploughman's in a pub,'
Nerissa said, and her aunt clucked her tongue.

'Is that all? Did you hear that, Philip? Isn't that
just like your father? John Thornton, you should
have taken her somewhere better than that. A bite
of cheese and some bread isn't a fit meal for anyone
but a mouse.'

'She said she wasn't hungry!'

'You shouldn't have taken any notice of her!'

Nerissa had stopped listening. She moved to the
bedside and looked down at Philip, her heart
wrung, wanting to cry. The top of his head was
bandaged, domed, only his face visible. He had
been shaved, she noted. There was no sign of
stubble on his cheek and she knew that Philip

needed to shave every day. He had once stopped shaving for a weekend camping trip on Hadrian's Wall, not far from his home, and come back on the Monday morning with the rough beginnings of a curly brown beard.

His mother wasn't talking any more. She was watching her niece. 'Say hello to him, Nerissa. He can hear you; they say he can, even if he isn't showing any signs. You know she's here, don't you, Philip? You're waiting for her to talk to you.'

His hand lay on the white coverlet, brown and strong, with wide-spanned fingers, nails cut very short, a practical hand used to hard manual work. Nerissa touched it lightly, whispered, 'Hello, Philip, it's me.'

'Say your name,' her uncle urged her. 'Say, it's Nerissa.'

'He knows,' Grace Thornton said, still watching Nerissa. 'I told him she was here, didn't I? Not that I needed to; he'll have known her voice the minute he heard it. We'll go and have a cup of tea, Nerissa, and leave you to talk to him.'

Nerissa didn't look round, just nodded. She heard them go out, heard the door click softly into place. She sank down on the chair her aunt had been sitting on and picked up Philip's hand, stroked it lightly.

'I'm sorry I haven't come until now. Your father only rang me yesterday.'

It had been one of the biggest shocks of her life. She had been at work, had picked up the phone expecting it to be a business call and heard her uncle's voice with a start of alarm. She had known it couldn't be good news; he wouldn't ring her at work for that.

'I came as soon as I could,' she added. She couldn't get over the blankness of his face. The emptiness. His features unmoving, unchanging.

This is how he would look if he were dead, Nerissa thought, and her body winced in pain. Maybe he is dying? If they switched off this life-support machine would he die?

'Darling, wake up!' Urgency possessed her. She was afraid to touch his face, afraid of jarring his head, so she put her face down against his hand and kissed it, held it to her cheek. She had half expected his skin to be cold but it was warm; she put her lips against his inner wrist and felt the blood pumping sluggishly there, in the blue vein which she could see threading beneath the skin.

'Wake up, Philip!' she whispered against this one sign of life in him.

There was no response, of course; she didn't expect any. He had lain like this ever since the car crash in which he had suffered head injuries necessitating surgery—surgery which had physically relieved the pressure on his brain, her uncle had told her, but had left him like this, in a deep coma.

She couldn't bear the idea of Philip dying. They had grown up together, as close as twins. For most of her life Philip had been the most important person in the world to her.

Behind her she heard the door open and sat up quickly, still holding his hand.

'You must be his cousin,' said a friendly voice and she turned to see a nurse behind her. 'Hello,

I'm his day special—I look after him during the day. He has someone else at night. I'm Staff Nurse Courtney.'

Nerissa smiled shyly at her. 'Hello.'

'How do you think he's looking?' The shrewd brown eyes watched her. 'Bit of a shock, I expect, seeing him like this, but his condition has stabilised; there's been no deterioration over the last couple of days.'

'Does that mean he's getting better?' Nerissa asked hopefully, and saw the other girl hesitate.

'Not exactly. It just means he isn't getting any worse, which, believe me, is a hopeful sign.'

Nerissa's face fell and Nurse Courtney quickly added, 'It could mean he is going to take a turn for the better any minute. His mother's doing a wonderful job and now you're here, too. Keep talking to him; he needs all the stimulation he can get, anything that keeps jogging his brain.'

She left a few minutes later and Nerissa sat down beside Philip again and took his hand. 'Do you like her?' she asked him conversationally. 'She has a very nice face—it matches her voice. I think you'll like her. She's the one who shaves you every day, she says. She's good at it, too; you couldn't do better yourself.'

His parents came back while she was telling him that it had started to rain. 'Typical—it was wonderful weather in London, but I get back here and down comes the rain! It's a wonder we don't all have gills and fins, the rain we get up here.'

John Thornton laughed behind her and she glanced round. 'Oh, your mum and dad are back, Philip.'

They sat down near by and talked to her, spoke to Philip as well, all the time, as if he were awake, so that after a while it seemed quite natural to Nerissa to do the same. She almost began to expect him to chime in occasionally—argue about something, laugh.

It had got dark by the time Grace Thornton looked at her watch and said, 'I think you should take Nerissa home for some tea, John. She's had a long journey today; she'll need a good night's rest.'

Nerissa couldn't deny she was tired—her eyelids were heavy and she had to suppress yawns all the time—but she protested. 'I went to stay, in case he wakes up!'

'You can't stay here all the time,' said his mother. 'It's exhausting. I should know; I've done it for hours at a stretch. But if you're to be any use to Philip you need to be fresh, and that means getting sleep. I shall be home later. I like to see him tucked up for the night, then I go home. We'll come back tomorrow morning.'

Nerissa fell asleep in the car during the drive through the hills to her uncle's farm. She woke up only when she heard dogs barking, and realised that the car had stopped in the farmyard.

'I thought I was going to have to carry you up to bed!' John Thornton said cheerfully. 'Grace was right. You're dead on your feet.'

'I think I'll go straight to bed,' she admitted, yawning. 'I'm not hungry.'

'You said that before,' he said, unlocking the solid oak front door and switching on the light in the small, panelled hall. 'Look, you get undressed

and hop into bed and I'll bring you some hot
chocolate and a sandwich—how's that?'

She hugged him. 'Oh, I've missed you, both of
you, in London! It's great to be home.'

She caught the flash of sadness in his eyes, and
knew what he was thinking. She couldn't let him
say anything, though, so she ran up the old,
creaking oak stairs, her nostrils filling with the
familiar fragrance from her childhood—beeswax-
polished furniture and stair-treads, home-made pot-
pourri from the roses and lavender in the garden.

This was not a large house but a solid, well-made
one, built of local stone and flint, carefully placed
to shut out the prevailing winds on these
Northumbrian hills, sheltered on all sides by ancient
trees and high stone walls. Lantern Farm had been
in one family since it was built in the seventeenth
century. The Thorntons were not rich but they had
always lived comfortably, running their sheep on
the pastures above the house, keeping a few pigs,
geese, horses and hens to supplement their income.

The furniture was all old, worn, shabby and well-
kept. It shone with polish. Any tears in curtains
and upholstery were neatly darned and there was
rarely need to buy anything since the attics were
well-stocked with household objects which were
often brought back into use when a fashion returned after a century or so.

There were four bedrooms. Nerissa had always
had a small one at the side of the house, overlooking an orchard. She undressed and climbed into
bed, shivering a little because it was so much colder
than her centrally heated home in London. At

Lantern Farm they still kept wood fires, and none
had been lit in this room since she'd left.

The faded tapestry curtains were threadbare; the
wind blew through the lattice panes and rattled the
door. On the bed lay an old patchwork quilt, made
by John Thornton's mother when she was first
married from dozens of little cut-up pieces from
old cotton shirts, dresses, curtains. The colours had
faded but Nerissa thought it was beautiful. She
stroked it, following the pattern, the diamonds and
circles interlocking, and then she looked around the
room, feeling very strange; it was like being caught
in a time warp, spun back to her teens, to a very
different Nerissa.

Her uncle arrived with a tray bearing a plate of
tiny, finger sandwiches—brown bread leafed with
ham and salad—a glass of water and a mug of hot
chocolate. Under his arm he carried a hot-water
bottle in a furry case which he handed her first.

'Oh, thank you,' she said gratefully, pushing it
under her covers and feeling warmth begin to cir-
culate around her frozen feet and legs.

'I should have lit a fire in here—shall I light one
now?'

'No, I'll be fine,' she said, and bit one of the tiny
sandwiches. 'Mmm, that's delicious. You remembered, I love ham.'

'Always did,' he said, beaming. 'Goodnight,
then, love. If there's anything you want, give me a
shout.'

Ten minutes later the light was out and Nerissa
was already half asleep.

It was strange to wake up in that house again.
Strange to put on jeans and a thick, warm sweater

and go out into the crisp autumn dawn where the shouting wind caught her black hair and blew it around her like a banner. She ran, startling horses in the pasture below the house. Climbing the wall and jumping down, she hunted for new mushrooms in the long grass where they had always grown.

When she went back to the house she found her aunt slicing tomatoes. 'I saw you from the window gathering mushrooms; we'll have them with toast,' Grace Thornton said. 'Your uncle's away up to the top, to work on one of the walls—it came down in the last storm. He took his breakfast with him and a flask of tea. There's nothing like rebuilding a wall to cheer him up.'

Nerissa remembered he had always gone off to work on the drystone walls whenever he was upset; the routine task was soothing to him.

After breakfast she and her aunt drove off to the hospital again. There was no change, Staff Nurse Courtney told them.

'No change isn't necessarily bad news, though,' she said, and Nerissa wished she could believe her. 'It's a long, slow haul,' added the nurse, and that, at least, Nerissa believed.

Towards the end of that very long day she wondered how her aunt managed to stay so cheerful, how she kept talking to her son when there was absolutely no response.

They had taken it in turns to talk to Philip. When his mother was tired she went off for a break and a cup of tea and sat outside, in the cool fresh air, in a little garden beside the ward, so that if she was wanted she was near by. Several times that day

Nerissa went out and left Philip alone with his mother. After sitting about for hours Nerissa preferred a brisk walk around the garden after she had had her tea and a sandwich.

Her uncle arrived in the afternoon, and at six o'clock Grace Thornton sent them both home again. 'And make sure you eat a proper cooked meal this time,' she told them. 'John, did you remember to pop that casserole into the oven?'

He nodded. 'Just as you said, at two o'clock. What time shall I take it out?'

'As soon as you want to eat. It won't spoil, but it's ready whenever you want it.'

When they got back to the farm Nerissa said, 'I'll serve supper,' but John Thornton shook his head.

'Nay, lass, your aunt told me to do it, and I'd better, or she'll never let me hear t'end of it.'

'I'll lay the table, then.'

They ate in the farm kitchen, the biggest room in the house, with white-washed deep stone walls, small windows, an old range which gave out great warmth on cold days and cheerful red and white checked curtains. The table was old and well-scrubbed, the wood deeply bitten with knife-cuts and scratches and carved initials. Along the high windowsills stood rows of pink geraniums, all grown by Grace Thornton, who often won prizes for them at local flower shows.

The casserole was lamb, with seasonal vegetables—potatoes and carrots, late green beans and leeks and onion. It was all grown there, on the farm, and the smell was mouthwatering and the taste delicious.

They washed up and put everything away, leaving some of the casserole in the oven for Grace when she got back. John Thornton went out to his yard to feed some of his animals, and Nerissa switched on the radio to listen to some music.

She curled up in a chair, her mind occupied with Philip, worrying, remembering his white face and the carved, blind look of his closed eyes.

Was he ever going to wake up? And, if he did, would he be some sort of human vegetable? She knew that that was what was terrifying his parents. They hadn't said anything, but she knew them. She had caught looks they gave each other, words they began and cut off.

She put her hands over her face. It wasn't fair! Why had this happened to Philip? Hadn't he borne enough grief already?

The phone rang beside her, making her jump. She had a sudden presentiment that it was news of Philip, that it was her aunt ringing from the hospital to say...what? That he had come out of his coma? Or...was dying?

Her hand shaking, she reached for it, whispered, 'Yes, hello?'

There was a silence at the other end.

'Hello? Lantern Farm,' Nerissa said urgently. 'Aunt Grace...is that you?'

The phone cut off suddenly. She held it, listening to the dead tone. Whoever had rung had hung up without speaking.

The silence was eloquent. Nerissa felt ice trickle down her nape. It could be a wrong number, of course. But she was afraid that it wasn't.

She was afraid it was Ben. He would have rung their home, only got the answering machine, then perhaps tried ringing friends, her boss. She had known that sooner or later Ben would realise she was not at home. She had hoped it would take him longer to work it out, but she had known it would happen, and that he would not forgive her for going to Philip without telling him what she meant to do.

Her heart beat with terror. If that had been him, what would he do now?

For the moment, nothing, she quickly told herself. He was in The Hague representing a client at the Court of Human Rights. He couldn't leave; this was an important case. Ben had been working on it for a long time; he wouldn't walk out on it now. He had said he estimated that it would take at least a week, maybe longer, for him to present his case. He wouldn't have to stay there to wait for the court's decision—that might take weeks, even months—but he certainly couldn't leave yet.

She had a breathing space. Days. Maybe a week, maybe longer. But sooner or later he would arrive and demand that she leave with him, and when she refused—as she knew she must—their marriage would be over.

CHAPTER TWO

NERISSA didn't sleep much that night, and when her aunt saw her next morning she gave her a frowning, anxious stare.

'You look terrible. Didn't you sleep? Your eyes look like holes in a white paper bag. I can't let you go to the hospital looking like that. They'll take one look at you and send you home in case you're coming down with something contagious.'

'I'm fine,' she said, sitting down at the table and looking without much interest at the fruit, the cereal, the coffee waiting for her.

'Fine? Nonsense!' snorted Grace Thornton. 'I know what you're like—if you're upset you don't sleep or eat and the next thing we'll find is that you're ill, too. Look what happened when you were competing in the county swimming competition— you couldn't stop throwing up for hours beforehand. And what about the year you took your final exams at school? You ended up with pneumonia that time. You're one of those people who can't take any sort of strain for long.'

Nerissa gave her a wounded look, her huge eyes darkened. 'I'll be OK. Don't stop me going to see Philip; I can sleep later, when I get back. That's all that's wrong with me—I had something on my mind and couldn't get to sleep for hours, that's all.'

Grace Thornton frowned, face intent. 'Something on your mind? What? Philip?'

'Of course. I can't help worrying about him, can I?'

'You mustn't let yourself worry; you have to be fit to sit by his bed all day. You must train yourself not to think too much.'

Nerissa laughed bitterly. 'That would be a good trick. Tell me how I do that!'

She poured herself some coffee, took one of the apples grown in the farm orchard—an old-fashioned, crunchy, brown-skinned russet—and bit into it, very aware of her aunt watching her.

'It isn't just Philip you've got on your mind, is it? What else is bothering you?' A pause, then Grace shrewdly said, 'Your husband?'

'Sometimes I think you're a witch,' Nerissa said, smiling wryly. 'How can you always read my mind?'

'I know you,' Grace said, and sighed. 'You should never have told him,' she added, her voice thickening with remembered pain and angry pride. 'I can't understand why you did, talking about family business to an outsider like that!'

Nerissa put down the half-eaten apple, her head bent, the cloudy dark hair falling in a wave over her face, hiding it from Grace.

'I didn't tell him. He guessed.'

A snort. 'How could he?' Grace rejected. 'He only spent two weeks up here and folk who've known us for years never guessed—how should he? What would he know about folk like us, and him coming from London, where they don't even know their own neighbour, let alone give them a helping hand when times are bad? Nay, lass, if he guessed you gave it away—you must have said something to give him a clue.'

'But I didn't *tell* him,' insisted Nerissa. 'He just picked it up from something I said, or read it in my face, or in yours... or...' Her voice faltered. 'Or in Philip's.'

Grace Thornton flinched, but said gruffly, 'I don't believe it. He couldn't have.'

Nerissa said flatly, 'Ben is very shrewd, especially with people. He's a lawyer, remember, trained to read character, to sense when people are telling the truth or lying—whether it's an out-and-out lie, or just not telling the whole truth. I never lied to him, I just... left out things... but all the same he guessed. It's as if he has antennae like a radio and can pick up what isn't being said, right out of the air.'

Grace Thornton's face had stiffened into a pale mask; she watched Nerissa bleakly. 'Aye, he doesn't miss a trick! A hard man—I could tell that from the minute he walked in here with you. I reckon they grow an extra skin in big cities like London, just to get by, like. It can't be easy living there, but I can't say I liked him. He's not our sort. But he is your husband; there's no getting past that.' She fell silent for a moment, then said quietly, 'Are you happy with him, Nerissa?'

She didn't ask, Do you love him, Nerissa? That was ice too thin for either of them.

Nerissa said, 'Yes,' quickly, too quickly.

Grace Thornton wasn't deceived. 'I'd feel a lot easier if I knew you were happy, love,' she said, and sighed.

Nerissa could never fool her. She had never known another mother; the bond of affection between her and Grace Thornton was very strong and sure, based on years of caring and security. There had been a time when it had been shaken, that trust—but its roots had been too deep and in time it had been rebuilt because of that long, deep affection.

Nerissa's parents had both died when she was very small—too young, in fact, to remember them clearly. Her mother had been Grace's sister, but they couldn't have been more different. Ellen had been tiny and delicate—it was from her that Nerissa had inherited her build and colouring. Ellen had died of leukaemia three years after her only child was born. Her husband, Joe, had taken Nerissa up to Northumberland to her aunt, and that was Nerissa's first memory—of being tired and weepy after a long journey from somewhere she didn't remember but later discovered to have been London, of wanting her mother, wanting her own home, being frightened and bewildered. Her father had carried her into the comfortable firelit kitchen and her aunt had taken her into her arms, kissed her, brushed back her black curls, murmuring to her, while over her shoulder Nerissa had stared down at Philip, who was almost a year older, but a sturdy little boy, much larger than herself, sitting on a rug playing with toy cars.

'That's your cousin; that's my Philip,' Grace Thornton had said. 'Go and play with him, sweetheart.' And she had set Nerissa down and given her a gentle push towards the other child.

Philip had grinned at her, silently held out one of his cars.

Nerissa had toddled over to take it and sat down on the hearthrug with a bump and had begun to push the car back and forward, making the same noises Philip was making. 'Brrmm...brrmm...'

She had never forgotten the moment. In a sense, it had been the beginning of her life. She couldn't remember anything that had happened before that moment, that day.

The first three years of her life had vanished—her mother's face, where they had lived—every detail. All gone, as if they had never happened.

Except that one moment, at the beginning, when she was carried into the firelit kitchen by her father. That instant was sharp and bright in her memory, beginning her conscious life.

Her father had left the next day and never come back. He had gone to Australia, she was told, and one day he would come back for her—but he never did. When she was seven she was told he had died, in the outback, of blood-poisoning, after neglecting a cut on his arm. There had been no doctor for many miles and it was too late by the time his condition was finally diagnosed.

Nerissa had cried when they'd told her, mostly because she felt she should, and even at the age of seven she'd had a strong sense of what she ought to do, think, feel. Her father's death had made no real difference to her life because by then she had felt she belonged here, with her uncle and aunt and Philip.

They were her family. She had forgotten she had ever had another one. Her life lay here, on the farm, in these remote, wind-blown hills. Their isolation threw them together more than most families; they had no near neighbours. There was another farmhouse half a mile away across the fields, but the farmer and his wife were old and their children grown-up and living away from home.

The nearest village was nearly two miles away, and it was tiny. It had a pub, a church which was hundreds of years old and a shop which sold anything and everything. Once there had been a school; it had closed years ago and now the children had to catch a bus to the next village which was larger and still had a school.

Nerissa and Philip had gone there, together, on the school bus which picked them up at the end of the lane running past the farm gates. In time they had both graduated to a large comprehensive, even further away, which meant a very long journey every day.

In the school holidays, and in the evenings and at weekends, they had helped on the farm, of course; Uncle John needed every spare hand he could get.

Farm work was hard, but it could be fun, too—helping to clear out ditches, cut back hedges, wheel barrows full of stones for mending drystone walls, prepare food for the various farmyard animals, muck out the stables, tramp the fields to check on sheep which had wandered and round them up with the help of the two sheepdogs.

Doing it alone wouldn't be so great, but when there were two of you—talking, playing jokes on each other, laughing—the time flew and you hardly noticed what you were doing.

There was always something new to do, too. Every day brought a new job—help to run the sheep through the bath of disinfectant every year, hold sheep for the vet while he injected them against the innumerable ills sheep were prone to, feed chickens or the few pigs they kept, whitewash outbuildings, slash back the nettles which invaded the yards if you didn't keep them down in summer.

Nerissa and Philip hadn't minded doing any of that. They'd enjoyed the variety of work on the farm; the jobs followed the seasons, changing all the time with the rhythm of the year.

Whatever they'd done, though, they'd done together. They'd always been together—inseparable—riding ponies across the fields to take them to the blacksmith to be shod, jumping walls and ditches, or in the summer lying in the sweet-smelling hay stored in the barn, talking and arguing, or in the fields, chewing ears of wheat and watching the poppies quiver in the warm air while Uncle John drove the harvester backwards and forwards across a field, and the blue sky wheeled overhead.

It seemed years ago. Nerissa winced, her blue eyes haunted by memories of how Philip looked now, how he had looked yesterday, in the hospital.

'I hate to think of him lying there, day after day! Philip always hated sitting still. He was full of energy.'

'Don't talk in the past tense!' snapped his mother. 'He isn't dead! And he isn't going to die, so stop talking like that!'

'I'm sorry,' Nerissa said. 'It's just...I feel so helpless. If only there were something we could do!'

'We're doing everything we can,' his mother said. 'Don't let it get to you, Nerissa. You won't help Philip by making yourself ill with fretting.' She smiled at her again, comfortingly, then looked at her watch. 'Let's be on our way.' She began to clear

away the breakfast things and Nerissa got up to
help.

Maybe there would be some change! she thought
as they drove to the hospital later. Sooner or later
he would open his eyes, surely! He must. He
couldn't stay the way he was, a living statue, locked
inside his own mind, dead to them.

But there was no change at all. That day was
much the same as the previous two had been. They
talked, while Philip lay unmoving, without expression. Nerissa read to him from the day's newspaper, began reading *Treasure Island* to him,
because it had always been his favourite book—he
had read it over and over again when he was a boy.

John Thornton arrived and spent an hour with
his son, then Aunt Grace sent them both back to
the farm.

'Go to bed and try to sleep, Nerissa,' she said as
they left. 'Promise me you will.'

'I'll see she does!' John Thornton said and his
wife nodded, patting his arm.

'Good lad.'

Nerissa watched and was overwhelmed with affection for her aunt; she was an astonishing woman,
proud and strong, and full of warmth and kindness.
She held them all together; without her they would
be lost.

When they reached the farm Nerissa made tea,
and she and Uncle John had a cup together in the
kitchen before he got up, sighing.

'A farmer's work is never done, especially if he
runs sheep!' he said. 'Stupid animals. I can't think
why I bother with them, sometimes.'

He tramped off into a rainy mist, which had come from nowhere, and Nerissa went up to her bedroom and found to her grateful surprise that Uncle John had lit a fire in the tiny grate. She stood in front of it and undressed down to her silky white slip, bra and panties, then lay down under the old, patchwork quilt, the curtains drawn, the fire dying down a little but a few flames still making black shadows climb the bedroom walls and the soft sound of rain soaking into the garden making a gentle lullaby.

A sound woke her. Her lashes fluttered, lifted. Drowsily she wondered what she had just heard— not a loud noise, a very quiet one. The sound of ash dropping through the fire grate? Or a log cracking apart in the flame? Her uncle's tractor far away on the hill?

What time was it? She rolled over to look at the clock and froze as she found herself looking into Ben's eyes. For a second she actually thought she was imagining it, calling him up from her unconscious because she was so terrified of seeing him again.

But she wasn't imagining anything. Ben was there, sitting beside her bed, and looking as if he had been there for some time, watching her while she slept.

Her body seemed to drain of blood. She stared into his eyes and felt like someone looking out into a winter landscape—grey and icy, impenetrable.

She was so stunned that she blurted out stupidly just what was on her mind. 'I thought you were going to be in The Hague for a week?'

The cold lips parted just enough to bite out a few words. 'So you hurried back to him.'

She winced as if at a blow from a lash. 'You don't understand——' she began, and was interrupted.

'Oh, I understand. You're still obsessed with him; you couldn't keep away.'

'No, you're wrong, I——'

His voice overrode hers. 'Have you been sleeping with him?'

'Philip's in hospital!' she shouted, sitting up, dragging the quilt with her to cover herself. 'He's in a coma; he doesn't even know I'm here.'

Silence. Ben stared fixedly.

She shrank back against the bedhead, went on flatly, 'He crashed his car nearly a week ago. His injuries were pretty bad. He wasn't wearing a seatbelt; his head was...' She swallowed, not bearing the idea of what had happened to his head. 'He had to have surgery to relieve pressure on the brain and he's been in a coma ever since. They can't say if...when...he'll wake up. It could be days, or weeks, or months—they just don't know.'

Ben's mouth indented. 'I'm sorry, I'd no idea,' he said in a low, harsh voice. 'No wonder you look like grim death.'

'We're all very worried, obviously,' she muttered, pushing back a strand of her dark hair which had strayed across her face. 'His mother's at the hospital with him, now—we've all been there, we go every day—but she sent me home early because she thought I looked tired.'

Ben's grey eyes roamed over her delicate face, bone-white at the moment except for the smoky shadows under her great blue eyes.

'That's why I was in bed at this time of day; I've been sleeping,' she added, very aware of his gaze and feeling her skin prickle with a familiar slow, sensual response. From the minute they'd met she had felt this unwanted reaction to him—not to the man himself, whom she had not even known at first, but to the male animal inside his expensive designer suit, to that powerful sexual mix of bone, muscle, flesh and dominating drive. Women always noticed Ben; she had seen it happen over and over again. The insistence of his personality made them gravitate towards him even in a crowded room. Nerissa had felt a strange pang many times as she'd watched his effect on other women, recognising it from her own first reaction to him.

It wasn't love, after all—how could it be? No, what she had felt—and still felt—was pure sexual desire, and she despised herself because it happened every time she saw him—even now, when she was so worried and unhappy over Philip.

She had always believed that you only felt like that about a man you loved. She wasn't sure yet exactly what she did feel about Ben, but she didn't think you could call it love.

Oh, he had become necessary to her—she wanted him, she thought about him when he wasn't there—but she didn't understand him the way she understood Philip. She didn't know him the way she knew Philip. The wordless, warm, certain love she had for Philip was a world away from the disturbing power Ben had over her.

If she could have married Philip... Her heart winced at the thought of how different her life would have been.

But fate had played a savage trick on them; they had been wrenched apart forever, with no hope of any future for them.

'How long have you been here?' Ben asked curtly, sitting down on the edge of her bed.

She couldn't meet his eyes. After a moment she whispered, 'Since the day you left for The Hague.'

A silence, then he bit out, 'They rang and told you about the accident after I'd left?'

She swallowed, cold sweat breaking out on her forehead. 'No, they rang me the day before.'

He didn't move or speak but the silence vibrated with violence. She sat there, trembling, afraid to look at him.

'And you didn't tell me.' His voice grated on her nerves; she wanted to scream, and couldn't. 'You let me leave, without saying a word, and as soon as I was out of the way you rushed up here without even leaving a note to tell me where you had gone.' He got up suddenly, walked across the room and back, and she picked up the simmering rage inside him.

This was the reaction she had been expecting. She knew how Ben felt about betrayal. His first wife had had an affair with his best friend for a year before Ben had found out. He had come home one day to find them in bed together. There had been a fight between the two men; Ben had put his 'friend' into hospital with a broken nose. Ben's wife had gone with the 'friend' in the ambulance after screaming abuse at Ben. Two years later Ben had divorced her; it had been another six years before he met Nerissa.

Nerissa knew he still carried the scars of disillusion and bitterness. Whatever he had been like before the day he'd come home to find his wife in bed with someone else, he was now a hard, remorseless man, determined never to let himself fall in love again. All he wanted from her was pleasure in bed. Love did not enter into their bargain.

He stopped at the bed and looked down at her, his eyes a blaze of rage. 'What were you going to do at the end of the week? Come back to me without ever mentioning that you had been away? Did you really think you could get away with it?'

'No, of course not! I knew you would find out but, anyway, Philip might be like this for weeks, months, and I——' She broke off, biting her lip.

'Didn't mean to come back at all,' Ben finished for her, his voice slow, his mind working all the time as he watched her. 'You're going to stay here,' he thought aloud. 'You never intended to come back to me.'

She clutched the quilt tighter, her small hands white-knuckled, her chin lifted and defiance in her eyes.

'He needs me,' she whispered. 'I can't leave him now, not like this, and it isn't just Philip—Aunt Grace and Uncle John need me, too. This has hit them pretty badly.'

Ben's mouth curled coldly, cruelty in the lines of it. 'Uncle John!' he repeated, and laughed.

'Don't!' she said, dark red invading her pale face, her eyes stricken.

Ben muttered under his breath and swung away again, walked back to the window, pulled aside the old tapestry curtain and looked out. A shaft of grey, rainy light entered the bedroom.

'Where are they both? I knocked on the front door but nobody answered, so I went round the back and the kitchen door was open, but there was no sign of anyone downstairs.'

'Aunt Grace is still at the hospital with Philip. Uncle John's somewhere on the farm, working. He has to spend so much time at the hospital, he has got behind with his work. He says he'll have to get someone to help out for a while, but the farm only just pays enough for the three of them to live on— it will be a drain on their budget to have to pay wages to an outsider.'

'And they hate outsiders, too,' Ben said in that cold, angry voice, swinging to face her.

She bit her lip. 'That's a bit over the top. I wouldn't say that; it's just that they...they are conservative.'

'They hated me from the minute they saw me!'

She pleated the quilt hem with her shaking fingers. 'That isn't true; they didn't hate you! They were...taken aback...when I brought you here. They hadn't expected——'

'You to find another man?'

'I was going to say someone like you!' she retorted, very flushed. 'Life here is so different from life in London. People like them...you just don't understand them; they're not like anyone you know.' Her eyes softened, her voice filled with affection and Ben watched her intently, frowning. 'They rarely meet strangers,' she said. 'They never go anywhere very much. Oh, they go to market once a month, they go to Durham to do Christmas shopping, but otherwise they almost never leave the farm. The furthest I can remember them going is to Scarborough, for a seaside holiday, and they don't do that every year even now, when Philip can take over and run things while they're away. They couldn't afford to go abroad. Hill farmers don't make enough money for foreign holidays. I don't think Uncle John has even been to London.'

Ben flared suddenly, his voice harsh. 'Why do you go on with this pretence? Isn't it time it all came out into the open? What the hell is the point in going on with these lies and half-truths? This whole business is so ingrown and contorted—if you once faced up to facts you might actually work out a few things about yourself.'

'Do you think I haven't?' she huskily threw back, looking up then, her eyes almost black with emotion in that white face. 'Once I knew . . . I realised I had to go away, and I did—you know that!'

Ben brooded on her, his face grim. 'How could they lie to you all these years? That's what I don't understand. The lies. Why couldn't they come out and tell you, years ago?'

'Pride,' she said, sadness in the line of her mouth, in her eyes. 'I said you didn't understand them. Can't you see? It was their pride that kept them from telling me.'

'Their pride?' exploded Ben. 'They cheated you for their own selfish reasons—you grew up unaware that you had a living father, not a dead one! If they had told you when you were small . . .'

'They couldn't bear to!'

'To hell with what they couldn't bear! What about you? Look what they did to you, with their pride and their lies! If they had ever cared twopence for you they'd have told you the truth years ago, and you would have been spared a lot of grief.'

'If they had known it was ever going to matter they'd have told me, but how could they guess? They couldn't see the future; they didn't have second sight.'

Ben's grey eyes flashed contemptuously. 'You're a born victim, aren't you? No matter what they did, you forgive them. Where's your pride, for heaven's sake? Where's your self-respect?'

Nerissa watched his hard, remorseless face and knew how he had looked when he'd seen his first wife, Aileen, in bed with her lover. Ben was not the forgiving type; from that instant his first marriage had been finished. And although he had told her, when they'd first met, the bare outline of what had happened he had never mentioned his first wife's name since. He had excised her from his life ruthlessly.

Nerissa was in no doubt that he would do the same with her. It would be easy enough; Ben had never been in love with her. She suspected that his capacity for love had died with Aileen's betrayal. One wound had been enough for Ben; he had made up his mind there and then never to let himself be vulnerable to such hurt again.

'I can't stop loving them just because they were human...' she whispered, making a helpless, confused gesture with her hands. The quilt slithered down, leaving her half naked, her shoulders bare, her breasts visible under the fine, cobwebby lace of her white slip and the delicate, lacy matching bra under that.

Ben's eyes focused. She heard his thick breathing and her own breathing quickened, her pulses beating a dangerous tattoo.

She hurriedly reached for the quilt again but Ben beat her to it, his long arm getting there first, tossing it on to the floor.

'Oh...' Nerissa wanted to protest but couldn't, not when he watched her with those glittering, hypnotic eyes.

He was suddenly very close, inches away. One long index finger reached out and touched her shoulder, slowly ran down her bare arm, tingling, making her blood run faster.

She knew what he was thinking about; she couldn't prevent her own desire leaping to meet his, her white face flooding with a tide of hot colour.

This was the only meeting-ground they had, this passionate, blind, instinctive heat. They had agreed from the beginning that love did not enter into their arrangement. Ben had been blunt about his reasons for wanting to marry her. He was a very well-known, highly respected lawyer. He had had one divorce, and it had been managed discreetly, without too much gossip, but he knew that for his career's sake he couldn't afford to get involved in any scandal, to be the object of rumour. He had been working obsessively for long hours ever since his divorce; Nerissa suspected he had been trying to forget, to bury his wife's memory. But Ben was also highly sexed, and a compulsive personality. His professional success was based on that drive to succeed, to conquer, to possess. It was that drive which had made him so fixated on having Nerissa. He had been brutally frank with her. He'd said he couldn't work or even think unless he had her, and not just now and then, on an occasional basis. Ben was also a possessive man. He couldn't bear the idea of her dating anybody else, ever belonging to anybody else. He had to be the only man in her life.

Yet he still had not talked about love, and that had made it easier for Nerissa to be equally frank with him. She had told him she had no love to give him, it had all been given long ago to someone else. But she liked Ben, she admired him—his strength of character, his dry humour, his intelligence, his cool control. If she hadn't liked him she could never have thought of marrying him. She hadn't needed to tell him that she could give him the physical satisfaction he craved, because Ben's mental antennae had picked that up long before; sometimes she almost thought he had known she wanted him before she had! The driving force of his passion gave her a release she needed desperately.

But she couldn't make love now. Not now, not here. How could he ask, expect her to?

In anguish she cried, 'No, Ben! Don't...I can't...'

Ben's face darkened, tightened. 'Under this roof, you mean?'

Nerissa flinched from his anger, then suddenly got angry too. How dared he look at her like that, talk to her in that contemptuous voice?

'Have you forgotten that Philip is desperately ill? How can you even think that I'd want sex now, when he may...any moment he...may die...?' Her voice broke and her eyes welled with tears.

She hated to show emotion in front of him; those cold eyes of his watched her with such remote distaste, as though her distress was somehow in bad taste. She covered her face with her hands and fought to get control of herself, choking back her sobs. Ben drew a harsh breath; his arms went round her, pulling her close. Nerissa fought him briefly, afraid he was going to try to make love to her, then she gave up because the effort sapped her reserves, made her cry harder. Ben's hand cupped her head, stroked her hair comfortingly, rhythmically, as if she were a child.

Once she realised there was nothing sensual in his touch she gave in, her body going limp, leaning on him, her hot, tear-stained face burrowed against his chest.

When her sobs died away and the tears stopped coming Ben tilted her head back with one finger under her chin and looked into her wide, wet eyes.

He bent and kissed her quivering lips gently. 'I'm sorry, Nerissa. I lost my temper. I forgot how ill he was and how upset you were.'

She didn't remember ever hearing Ben apologise before. He might mock her family's pride, but Ben's pride was every bit as stiff-necked; he was a hard, assured man who disliked losing a case or an argument.

Huskily she said, 'Please try to understand! It's been such a strain, Ben. If there were only something we could do, but we just have to sit there and watch him all covered in tubes and wires, bandaged up like an Egyptian mummy, looking——' She broke off, gestured wildly. 'It isn't him in that bed; it isn't Philip—he's somewhere else, far away from us all, and we can't reach him. His mother sits there talking and talking and he can't hear her, although she is so sure he can...it breaks my heart to watch her, it's all so useless.'

'Not necessarily,' Ben said soberly. 'I gather that stimulation is what a coma patient needs—familiar voices, favourite music, the TV programmes they like—it all helps. And as for your aunt—well, I'm sure it is helping her to be with her son and talk to him, whether he can hear or not. You may not think she is doing anything useful, but she believes she is, and that must be a comfort to her. So, either way, her long chats with him are certainly not a waste of time.'

'Yes, of course,' she said with a tired sigh. 'I know all that with my head, but...oh! I suppose I'm afraid to hope.'

His eyes watched her, bleak as winter. 'You've learnt not to,' he interpreted, deadly accurate as usual. She had told him very little about herself; she couldn't understand how he managed, all the same, to work out what she was thinking.

'Fate hits you out of nowhere and there's nothing you can do,' she murmured, staring at nothing, her face drawn and pale again.

Quietly, Ben said, 'That was what I was trying to make you see—if they had told you when you were a child you would never have got hurt the way you did. It was all avoidable. Their pride was what hurt you—not fate.'

'Maybe,' she admitted, her head bent and her ruffled black hair falling over her face. 'But they're human, they aren't perfect—I never said they were. The point is they did their best, in difficult circumstances, and I admire them for the way they coped with such a terrible dilemma.'

'Who created the dilemma?' Ben grated and she sighed.

'I know. And for a while I was bitter, and angry, but you can't turn love off, like water in a tap. I still loved them. When I thought about it more calmly, I understood why they did what they did. I couldn't refuse to forgive them, especially as it would hurt Aunt Grace and I couldn't bear to hurt her of all people.'

'Your aunt is extraordinary,' Ben agreed, his face very serious. 'In her place I don't think I'd have behaved so well. She's some sort of saint. But I still say you should have been told, and to hell with their pride.'

She shot him a charged look. 'But then you're perfect, aren't you, Ben? You never make mistakes, you never hurt anyone, you never do anything stupid or wrong. It must be wonderful to be so perfect but ordinary people rarely manage it. They blunder through life trying to do what is right and failing all the time because their humanity gets in the way.'

His black brows jerked together, his grey eyes dark with anger. 'You don't like me much, do you?'

She defiantly met his glare. 'Not much, right at this moment, no!'

His voice was harsh. 'Well, that's too bad, Nerissa. But, like me or not, you're my wife and you're going to stay my wife. You're coming back to London with me.'

She had been expecting this demand and tensed to meet it. 'They need me! I can't leave them to cope with this on their own!'

His face was taut, his eyes hard. 'You can stay a few more days, but I'm staying with you. I'm not leaving you here, alone.'

His anger made her skin throb as if it bruised her. If he stayed she knew what it would mean— he intended to share this room with her, this bed. He would insist on making love to her and she couldn't bear the idea.

'Philip may not come out of his coma for months! I can't go back to London, leaving him like that.'

'You aren't staying up here alone for months! Do I have to remind you that it was me you married, not him?'

'I want a divorce, Ben!' she broke out in a voice that shook, and the room filled with an intolerable tension.

He frightened her when he looked like that; there was cruelty in his mouth, in the clenched jawline.

'I'll fight it,' he said curtly. 'I'll use any weapon I have to—even if it means bringing him into it. What do you think that will do to your family pride?'

CHAPTER THREE

NERISSA was appalled and sat staring at him in a state of shock. 'You wouldn't,' she whispered at last.

Ben's face was fierce, his eyes stabbing her. 'Why shouldn't I? It would be the truth.'

'That's a lie! I've been totally faithful to you since we got married!'

'That depends what you mean by faithful! Oh, physically, no doubt you have.' His mouth twisted in cold cynicism. 'I've kept you far too busy in bed to have the energy to spare for anyone else.'

She was hot again, blushing to her hairline.

'But there are other ways of being unfaithful, Nerissa, aren't there? You betrayed me in your heart, every day of our marriage.'

'You knew, before we got married, how I felt. I told you I didn't love you.'

His eyes flickered; he frowned, his mouth tightly reined. 'Maybe I thought that in time you'd forget him, but you didn't, did you?' His voice deepened, grated. 'Every time I took you in my arms I know he was in the bed with us! He was always there, between us. I got the distinct feeling that you were even guilty because you were in my bed—you felt you were being unfaithful to him!'

She flinched. How did he do it? He kept reading her most secret thoughts, as if he could walk in and out of her head.

Ben watched her, his eyes cynical. 'Yes. I thought so,' he said through his teeth. 'The only way I could drive him out was to make love to you so hard you couldn't think of anything at all!'

She trembled, remembering those nights when his passion was almost brutal.

'And you always responded,' Ben said, his mouth twisting. 'You can't deny that.'

No, she couldn't deny it. In fact, she had almost needed it, that desire which verged on the barbaric, driving their bodies into a frenzy of sensuality.

Watching her flushed face, Ben went on. 'And now you want me to let you go, so that you can come back here to him! I'm stunned you actually think I might let you go! I kept my side of our bargain—I never asked you for love and I'm not asking you for it now, but I still want you, Nerissa. I haven't tired of your body yet. You aren't walking out on me.'

'You can't drag Philip into a divorce case!' she half pleaded, half accused. 'It would be a lie, and you know it.'

'I'm not going to claim that you and he are lovers,' Ben said curtly. 'I only have to tell the truth—that you're in love with him, and have left me to go back to him and live under his roof.' He paused, then added with deadly quietness, 'And then I would have to explain why I find that so disturbing.'

She looked at him in horror, stricken. 'You couldn't! It would destroy them to have it talked about in open court!'

He was unmoved. 'Then don't mention divorce again.'

Downstairs they heard a bang, the sound of movements, then feet creaked on the worn old treads of the staircase.

'Your uncle?' Ben murmured, getting up.

She had to swallow on what felt like broken glass before she could answer. 'Probably.' Her voice sounded so normal; she couldn't understand how she could talk at all. She slid out of the bed in a hurry, almost fell over, recovered her balance and grabbed at her dressing-gown. Ben watched her put it on without attempting to help, for which she was grateful. She did not want him touching her. Her stomach churned at the very idea.

She turned towards him, tying her belt with trembling hands. 'Don't tell him what we've been talking about...don't say anything to him about divorce!'

Ben's eyes were hooded; he didn't answer and a second later they heard John Thornton's footsteps right outside, then his tap on the bedroom door.

'Nerissa? Are you awake? There's a strange car parked outside; has anyone come to the house?'

She walked over and opened the door. 'Ben's here,' she told him, and saw the surprise in his face.

'Oh. It's Ben's car?' He looked past her. 'Hello there, Ben, how are you?'

They were still semi-strangers, these two men, although Ben was her husband. The two weeks Ben had spent here before they'd got engaged had been intended as a chance for her family to get to know him, but it had been Ben who had learnt most. He was so quick to pick up atmosphere, to tune into what people were feeling or thinking—what was really going on in a situation. It hadn't taken him long to work out the tangle in her family.

Her family, though, were slow, country people— quiet, rooted, thoughtfully turning over what they noticed and digesting it before they reached a conclusion. They had not taken to Ben. He was a city man, a foreigner, not versed in their way of thinking. Perhaps they had hoped that Nerissa, if she married, would choose someone of their own sort, not this clever, disturbing stranger.

Watching them as they formally shook hands, Nerissa suddenly realised that oddly enough there was a certain similarity between Ben and her uncle. They were much of a height and of the same physical type—tall and loose-limbed, wide-shouldered, slim-hipped. The differences were more subtle—Ben had a drive John Thornton lacked, his eyes were sharper, clearer, his face harder, the mouth and jaw an expression of formidable will.

'I'm sorry to hear the news about your son,' Ben said. 'You must be very worried.'

John Thornton nodded unsmilingly, and she sensed that he resented Ben discussing Philip, did not want to talk about his son to this stranger who had married Nerissa. 'Aye,' he said shortly, then changed the subject. 'Nerissa told us you were in The Hague for a week—something about a foreign court case?'

'The Court of Human Rights,' Ben said shortly. 'The case was adjourned for further reports. After the first day's hearing they decided there was an angle that needed further reports, and the other side have got to provide documents they want to see. I shall have to go back there in a month or so. If we're lucky. Even if the other people come up with the required documentation, European bureaucracy works so damn slowly that it could be a long time before we get another slot in the schedule.'

'Seems to me the law always works damn slow,' said John Thornton.

Ben smiled coldly. 'I'm afraid so.'

Again John Thornton changed the subject. 'Have you eaten? I was just about to serve the supper—my wife left a casserole in the oven for us. It's nothing special, just chicken and vegetables—there's more than enough for three, though, and my wife is a very good cook.'

'Thank you, I'd like that,' Ben said, but before John Thornton turned away to go back downstairs he said, 'As I haven't any other commitments in London for the rest of this week, I'd like to stay here, if that won't be too much trouble for you. I know Nerissa won't want to leave while your son is still so ill, and as she's under such a strain I feel I should be here with her. I realise that at a time like this you already have a lot on your plate; I don't want to be in the way or add to your workload. Why don't Nerissa and I move to the village pub? I remember they have a couple of rooms they let to visitors.'

John Thornton frowned. 'We couldn't have you and Nerissa doing that!' He looked wryly at Ben. 'It'd make tongues wag in the village! Nay, lad. You'll stay here; there's plenty of room.'

'Thank you,' Ben said in that polite, formal voice. 'I'm sure you're right. It might cause talk if we stayed elsewhere. I'll make myself useful while I'm here, then. I can cook and wash up, even push

a vacuum cleaner around the house or feed some
of your animals, if you show me how.' He smiled
at the older man. 'I have to point out, though, that
the bed in this room is not big enough for two!'

Nerissa went pink.

John Thornton looked across the room at the
bed, made a face. 'You're right, it isn't, is it?'

'It wouldn't be too comfortable, the two of us
squashed into a bed that size!' Ben murmured and
John Thornton laughed.

'We'll soon do something about that. There's
plenty of space for another bed in this room and
there's one in the spare room—it hasn't been used
for a while but we can air it in front of the fire for
a few hours, then you can push both beds together.
How's that?'

Nerissa bit down on her inner lip to choke back
the cry of protest threatening to escape.

She was helpless; Ben knew she dared not say
anything with her uncle there, listening. She was
terrified of bringing the reality of the situation into
the light, and he knew it.

Blandly, he smiled at John Thornton. 'Thank
you, that would be fine. Can I help you get the bed
in here?'

'Thanks, I could do with a hand—the bed's
brass, and heavy. We'll do it now, shall we? Nerissa,
make up the fire, love. It has almost gone out!'

John Thornton and Ben left the room and she
went over to the fireplace, gently raked the ash and
dying embers, chose a couple of the logs from the
old wicker log-basket on the hearth and settled them
into place in the grate, picked up the ancient leather
bellows which hung from a hook in the fireplace,

knelt down and began to blow some life back into the fire. The men came back into the room just as a bluish flame shot up, licking along the dry logs which began to crackle and burn, drops of golden resin forming on their surface.

Nerissa arranged the bedroom chair in front of the fire, at a safe distance, and the mattress was propped up in front of it. Then the men worked together setting up the brass bedstead. It was Victorian and its brasswork was worn with years of polishing; it shone like gold in the growing fire-light. The flames were now shooting up from the logs with a crackling, spitting sound and the room was much warmer.

When the bed was set up John Thornton stood back, nodding. 'That should do. Nerissa knows where my wife keeps the linen. I'll get back down and see about the casserole. Best get dressed, Nerissa—can you both come down in ten minutes?'

He left, closing the door behind him, and she felt her nerves prickle as she was left alone with Ben in the room he fully intended to share with her from now on.

He threw himself down full-length on her bed, his dark head propped up on his hands, watching her lazily.

'Why don't you go down and have a drink before supper?' she asked him and he smiled, a slow, sardonic twist of the mouth.

'I'd rather watch you get dressed.'

Angrily, she broke out, 'Well, I don't want you watching me!'

'I know that,' he drawled.

Flushed, she muttered, 'Aren't I entitled to a little privacy?' She grabbed up some clothes, made for the door.

'Where are you going?' Ben was off the bed and between her and the door in a flash, his lean, agile body moving at tremendous speed.

She halted, her face mutinous. 'To the bathroom.'

He pulled the clothes out of her hands before she could stop him. 'You can go to the bathroom, but you must come back in here to get dressed.'

'Why are you doing this?' she flared, her eyes fever-bright with irritation. 'You've seen me get dressed and undressed a hundred times. Why insist on watching me now?'

His eyes held hers, insistent, cool, mocking. 'Because you don't want me to.'

She caught her breath, her lower lip worried between her teeth.

Ben said drily, 'When we first got married you were very shy and inhibited, but we got over that stage, didn't we? For months now you haven't minded my seeing you naked, and you've stopped blushing every time I take my clothes off in front of you. Suddenly, now you're back here, you revert to the way you were six months ago. And we both know why, don't we?'

She couldn't bear to talk about it any more. She ran instead—ducked past him and pulled the door open, afraid that at any moment he might stop her. But he didn't. He stood and watched her as she rushed out.

Safely locked in the bathroom, she sat on the edge of the white-enamelled bath and contemplated her situation with a rising sense of panic. Ben was remorseless, unforgiving. He was going to inflict punishment on her for what he saw as infidelity, a betrayal of the heart if not the body.

She knew how he felt about betrayal. From the dark glitter of his eyes she realised with foreboding that the wound to his pride had gone deep, almost as deep as the wound his first wife had given him.

Ben hated the idea of people laughing at him, especially now that he was a famous name. He had been the object of a lot of press interest in the past few years because he had fought some very famous cases, including the defence of a woman charged with the murder of a brutal husband. That case had hit the headlines for weeks: Ben's compelling defence of his client had made very good copy for reporters and when he'd got married himself, not long afterwards, that had made the papers too. Their marriage had caused a lot of speculation among his friends as well; they had all expected him to marry someone from his own world, with money or position, who could help him in his rise to the top. Nerissa was a complete shock to them. She was an unknown, without money or fame; she didn't fit into his world.

But Ben had married her, ignoring the reactions of everyone around him. Now, if she walked away from him and their marriage, he would feel humiliated, and no doubt there were some people who would laugh at him behind his back. Ben would hate that. Ben hated failure; he couldn't bear not to win in court—he would fight grimly to the last second in order to get a verdict for his client.

This time he was his own client, and he needed to win for even more complex reasons than usual.

She looked at her reflection in the bathroom mirror; her eyes were shadowed with pain and fear and distress. I didn't lie to him! she thought angrily. I told him I didn't love him when he asked me to marry him. And when he guessed about Philip he said he understood and wouldn't ask for anything I couldn't give; he wanted my body, not my heart. He never pretended to love me, either.

Why can't he let me go?

His ego! she thought. His precious ego! He was afraid of losing face. Ben Havelock, the great lawyer, mustn't be made to look a fool. He had a very strong sense of identity. With good reason. He was a public figure with, unquestionably, a great career in front of him. 'The silver-tongued crusader,' one newspaper had dubbed him a few months back, when he'd won a case for which he'd only got the pittance allowed under legal aid, but which Ben had taken because he had been moved by the plight of a child.

She couldn't deny that Ben had a heart as well as a brain—professionally he was at his most brilliant when he was dealing with human emotions which had somehow led to a client being dragged into the labyrinth of the law—but his emotions had never been involved in their marriage. What he had wanted—and she had given—was the hot sensuality of their nights together.

Her eyes shifted away; she frowned. All that was perfectly true but there was one aspect of the truth she wasn't admitting, and she knew it.

When she had got the call telling her that Philip was so ill she hadn't told Ben because she had been afraid he would order her not to come. Her instincts, her female intuition, had warned her that Ben was going to resent the idea of her rushing off to Philip's bedside whether he was seriously ill or not. That was why she hadn't said anything, why she had come secretly, knowing that sooner or later Ben would realise she wasn't at their home and find out where she had gone.

In working out Ben's probable reactions she had guessed that he was going to be bitterly angry with her, but she had been very wrong about what he would do when he did find out. She had believed that he would end their marriage there and then, tell her not to come back, divorce her. She had thought his pride would make him break with her— but his pride was having a very different effect.

Her blue eyes met their reflection in the mirror. She was flushed again, her features tense. What about herself? What did she want?

After all, nothing had changed. The bedrock of her situation remained the same. She had married Ben because she was lonely, she felt lost in London and knew very few people ... Her blue eyes flashed angrily at their reflection. And because you wanted him! she mocked herself. Why pretend you didn't?

Every time he kissed you, touched you, made love to you, you wanted it more.

Pleasure, she had discovered, was addictive. While she was in Ben's bed she could forget everything else. In the little death of orgasm she was taken into sweet oblivion for a while until it was over and she had to come back down to earth, and remember.

It might not seem a very good reason for marrying someone she didn't love. But her future had seemed so bleak, so empty, and Ben had offered her a home, companionship as well. And, after all, she was cut off from the man she did love by an unbridgeable abyss. She couldn't marry him, and she'd known she would never want to marry anyone else for love. Love would never again be one of her options.

She never wished to fall in love again. She had said so to Ben, and he had told her he felt the same. His first marriage had cured him of falling in love. They really had a lot in common, he had said drily.

So she had said yes to Ben and it had worked out, just as he had prophesied. So far.

They were both very involved in their jobs. Ben had to work hard, late into the night at times; he was often away from home. He kept his social life to the minimum but liked having Nerissa as his hostess, was always generous in buying her designer clothes to wear on special occasions, often brought her flowers, and when a case ended in his client's favour Ben usually bought her a piece of jewellery to celebrate.

Nerissa's job was not quite as spectacular, but she enjoyed it and earned a very good salary. She worked for a firm which specialised in office design. Nerissa was a glorified salesgirl, in fact. She was sent out to look at a new client's offices, to show him a portfolio, talk him through what he wanted and how the design firm could supply it and, hopefully, take a firm order. She would take all the necessary measurements, and then the design team would draw up a finished plan. When the client had approved that and the fittings had arrived in due course, the firm sent in its specialist team to fit the office.

Ben wasn't so sure he liked her job or what it entailed. Nerissa needed to be warm, friendly, sympathetic, understanding.

'They use you as bait,' Ben had once said in a hostile voice. 'You're there to seduce the client. That's why they don't use men. Change your job, Nerissa. It isn't right for you.'

But she enjoyed the job and liked the people she worked for; her days were as busy as Ben's and she was never bored.

They had achieved a fragile understanding over these months. Philip's accident had wrecked it overnight. If he recovered she would stay to help his parents, to help look after him, but in the long run she couldn't stay here; she would have to leave again, eventually.

But for what? Life alone again, with all that meant? London must be the loneliest place in the world. Nerissa was shy and found it hard to make friends. She had hated living alone in a big city, brushing shoulders with strangers day after day, going home to a tiny, empty flat, lying alone in the dark, afraid of every noise, every shadow.

What alternative did she have, though? Go back to Ben? She groaned aloud, staring at herself in the mirror as though trying to read in her eyes what she really thought, really wanted.

Ben had said things just now that disturbed her, worried her. She still didn't really know him, did

she? There was that darkness in him, that secret
barbarity, which ran deeper than she had suspected.

Oh! What was the point in thinking about all
this? She didn't know. She couldn't make up her
mind what to do—it could wait, it would have to
wait, until Philip came out of his coma. If he came
out of it, her mind added, flinching at the thought.

Hurriedly she washed, cleaned her teeth, brushed
her hair, then went back to the bedroom.

Ben lay on the bed again, his long body casually
at ease. Her clothes had been neatly folded over
the end of the brass bed.

Averting her eyes from her husband, Nerissa went
to pick them up then sat down on a chair to change
into clean tights and panties before taking off her
dressing-gown. Ben watched her. She felt like hitting
him; the provocative gaze made her skin prickle.
Oh, ignore him! she told herself. He's only doing
it to get at you; don't let him succeed.

She shed her dressing-gown, stood up to put on
a black pleated skirt and pink sweater. As she
buckled a black leather belt around her slender
waist Ben clapped slowly, sarcastically.

Nerissa flung him a furious glance.

'Not the best performance in the world—it could
have been sexier, less inhibited—but I enjoyed it,'
he mocked.

'Oh, why don't you leave me alone?' she seethed.

His eyes glittered. 'I'll never do that, Nerissa,
not while I still want you in my bed.'

They starred at each other, like duellists across
drawn swords, and yet with that constant, mad-
dening flicker of sexuality between them, as if the
shadowy room were lit with lightning, not firelight.

'And I want you,' Ben whispered, sending a shiver of arousal down her spine. 'Now, Nerissa, I want you now.'

From downstairs John Thornton called. 'Supper's on the table! Come and get it!'

Nerissa silently made for the door, for the stairs, almost running, trying not to remember what Ben had just said. He followed slowly, his feet light on the worn old treads of the staircase. Having him here, under this roof, made her feel so strange. His presence interfered with her memories of all the years gone by when she and Philip had run up and down these stairs, escaped out into the moors and hills. Those years lay in her mind like a pool of clear, pure water; Ben's reflection broke up the surface, superimposed his image on her memories of Philip.

Was it deliberate? she wondered. Was that what he wanted to do? Was it why he had followed her here? She was beginning to think it was. In the beginning, when he'd first found out about Philip, long before they'd got engaged, he had seemed very cool and understanding about the way she felt. He had assured her that he didn't care if she loved someone else—all he wanted from her was pleasure in bed.

She didn't suppose for a second that he was in love with her himself—no, it was black pride that drove Ben, not love. She was his wife now. He expected to own all of her—body and heart, soul and mind. The wife of Ben Havelock must not let her mind stray to other men, or threaten Ben's worldly position in any way. She might threaten divorce, but she was certain he would hate it—not only the publicity—although it could damage his career if he was divorced a second time—but also the idea of everyone knowing another woman had left him for someone else.

'There you are!' her uncle said, looking round. 'Come on, before this food gets cold!'

'Sorry,' she mumbled, sitting down at the table and as she smelt the food realising she was hungry. 'Mmm...wonderful smell...'

'Grace makes a good chicken casserole.' He looked at Ben proudly. 'My wife is a marvellous cook.'

'Your wife is a marvellous woman,' Ben said with a sardonic undertone.

John Thornton stiffened, flushed, shot a look at Nerissa, his eyes reproachful. She couldn't answer that look, not in front of Ben, couldn't say, I didn't tell him, he guessed, and I'm so sorry!

After a charged silence John Thornton nodded, said in a dignified voice, 'She is that; you're right.' He gestured to their plates and the casserole dish covered in the centre of the table. 'Help yourselves...'

They ate in the kitchen by candlelight; the casserole was perfectly cooked, the chicken tender and delicately flavoured with the onion, carrots, leeks and herbs with which it had been slowly cooking and served with wild rice and peas.

Ben insisted on clearing the table and putting the washing-up into the machine while Nerissa made coffee for them all. As they were drinking their coffee Grace Thornton arrived back and stopped in startled surprise at the sight of Ben.

'Well, I never did!'

He got up to kiss her cheek. 'Hello, Grace, how are you?'

'I shall survive,' she said, shrugging. 'Nerissa didn't tell us you'd be coming up here. She said you were abroad, working.'

'I was. My case in The Hague was postponed so I came up here to join Nerissa. I'm very sorry to hear about your son's accident—how was he when you left him?'

She recovered quickly, smiling at him with a weary face. 'No change, I'm afraid, but they seem quite pleased with his condition, apart from the coma. If we can only make him wake up they say he would soon be on the road to recovery. Physically, he has coped very well with the surgery.' She looked around the immaculate kitchen. 'Have you had your supper?'

'Yes, it was delicious—perfectly cooked—and Uncle John made wild rice and peas to go with it,' said Nerissa. 'We left some for you; it's in the oven. Sit down, Aunt Grace. I'll get it for you.'

With a sigh Grace Thornton sat down and Nerissa deftly served her the rest of the chicken casserole with the speckled wild rice and green peas which perfectly complemented the pale golden colour of the fowl, the green leeks and orange carrots.

Her aunt inhaled the scent of the food, sighing. 'I just realised I'm starving.'

'You look tired,' said Ben, and Grace looked at him wryly.

'Dead on my feet. And I haven't done anything all day, that's the irony of it. Just sat in a chair by his bed, talking.'

Ben laughed, but said gently, 'Stress is a killer, you know. You ought to get more rest, spend a little less time at the hospital.'

'That's what I keep telling her,' John Thornton said at once. 'She can't keep it up like this forever.'

'I'm fine,' his wife dismissed.

'What would happen to your son if you collapsed too?' said Ben, and Grace Thornton shrugged that away too.

'I shan't.'

Ben considered her, his dark head on one side, then smiled with sudden warmth at her. 'No, you're tough, aren't you?'

She laughed. 'I've needed to be.'

John Thornton drew an audible breath, his face tight.

'I'd better go up and make your bed,' Nerissa hurriedly told Ben without looking at him. 'The mattress should be well aired by now.' She glanced at her aunt, explaining, 'We took the brass bed from the spare room. The mattress has been standing in front of the fire for the last couple of hours.'

'Wait till I've finished my supper and I'll give you a hand making the bed,' Aunt Grace said, but Ben was on his feet.

'I'll help her; you stay there and rest,' he said. 'I've had a long drive up here from London and I think I'll go straight to bed. Goodnight.'

Nerissa huskily said, 'Goodnight,' too, avoiding their eyes as if she was afraid they might read in her own eyes what she was thinking.

The moment had come; the night was upon her. Panic and wild excitement duelled in her blood. She was afraid of Ben, and she wanted him, but above all she was uneasy about making love to him under this roof.

This house was Philip's home. They had never made love here. She didn't think she could bear to, not with Philip close to death and memories crowding in on her like moths on a flame.

She found the sheets and pillowcases, smoothly ironed and scented with lavender, in the linen cupboard, and she and Ben silently worked together to make the bed, then Nerissa collected her night-dress and went to the bathroom to wash and clean her teeth.

Ben surveyed her ironically as she returned, his gaze flicking down over the demure white cotton nightdress, Victorian in style, with a high neck and low hemline trimmed with lace.

'Don't go to sleep, I'll be back in a minute,' he drawled as he went out to the bathroom in his turn.

Nerissa put the light out and snuggled down under the covers, pulling them right up to her chin, then turned over to face the wall so that her back would be towards Ben when he came back.

She had hardly had time to settle when the door opened again. Ben stopped dead, seeing the light out, and then he closed the door very quietly. Nerissa's heart began to beat so fast she felt sick. She lay in the dark, listening intensely, as he walked across the room.

He trod softly between their two beds and for a second she thought he was going to get into his own bed, but then he sat down on the edge of hers.

'Your bed or mine?'

The hair on the back of her neck stood up. Huskily, she whispered, 'I'm nearly asleep, I'm so tired, Ben. Not tonight, please.'

'Move over,' he simply said, then pulled back the covers and slid in beside her.

· She quivered at the contact of that warm, male body close behind her. He came closer, his arms going round her waist. He was nuzzling her neck, pushing aside her clouds of dark hair to kiss the sensitive skin of her nape, and her nerve-ends prickled with awareness of him, an awareness that quickened when his hands softly moved upwards, cupped her breasts, the heat of his palms permeating the fine cotton of her nightdress.

Her mouth went dry. Her eyes closed; she was trembling, heat growing between her thighs.

She wanted him; she always did when he touched her. Her body found him irresistible. But if he made love to her here, tonight, in this room, in Philip's home, she recognised, it would destroy the delicate balance of her life.

It was one thing to marry Ben, to live with him, sleep with him every night, in London. London was another world, another planet. What happened there didn't impinge on this place.

This was where she and Philip had grown up. It was a precious glass globe holding an entranced world which would never change, would always be the same—a remembered happiness which was both real and illusory.

If Ben made love to her tonight he would smash that globe; life would break in on that entranced world and she couldn't bear that to happen.

Anger surged up in her and she tore herself out of Ben's arms, sat up, leaned over and snapped on the bedside lamp.

Ben lay still, watching her, his eyes narrowed and intent, hard and bright as polished silver.

'I told you! I don't want to make love tonight!' Nerissa told him hoarsely.

'Well, I do,' Ben said through his teeth. His long arm shot out and switched off the light again; the darkness enveloped her, shot through with threat and a pulsing sensuality. 'And just for once,' Ben said harshly, 'I'm not sharing my bed with your dream lover! Tonight it is just going to be me and you!'

As he reached for her Nerissa tried to scramble away, but Ben was too quick. He pulled her down; his body rolled on top of her. She gasped at the impact of his weight, and a second later Ben's mouth hit hers.

Her lips were parted in that gasp; she couldn't stop him invading between them. She couldn't fight the fierce, insistent demand of that long kiss—he was almost suffocating her; her head was swimming; she was half fainting.

His hands slid down her body, exploring her under the soft folds of her nightdress; he pushed it up and touched her intimately, his fingertips teasing, tormenting her.

Nerissa cried out under his mouth, arching helplessly, the prisoner of her deepest instincts. Ben had been her lover for months now; he was as familiar with her body as she was. He knew precisely how to touch her, how to arouse her sensuality, make her respond to him, and her breasts were full and aching as he kissed them, her nipples dark-ringed, erect.

He lifted his head, stared down at her with glittering eyes, his breathing thick and impeded.

'Now tell me you don't want me!'

She was incapable of saying anything, trembling, flushed and breathless, and Ben didn't wait for her to pull herself together.

He was naked now; he came down on to her again, kneeing her legs apart, moving between them, his body urgent. His hands slid over her buttocks, caressing, stroking; he lifted her, entered her, and Nerissa gave a wild groan, her body arching instinctively to take him.

From the very beginning it had been like this— the very sensation of having him inside her made her feel completed in a way that she could never understand but couldn't deny or argue against.

She might love someone else but her body needed Ben, as if he was a missing part of her, necessary to make her whole again. She had often despised herself for feeling like that about someone she did not love the way she loved Philip; she couldn't understand why Ben could always do this to her in spite of her mind saying no, but it happened every time—it happened now.

He moved on her, in her, driving for satisfaction with unleashed barbarism, his demand reaching a primitive core inside Nerissa which matched his— the more fiercely he drove into her, the wilder the pangs of pleasure inside her grew. She met his deep intrusions, pulled him closer, her arms around his back, her hands gripping him, her nails digging into him. When they made love there were always nailmarks on his back afterwards; the first time it had happened she had been appalled, shocked and incredulous, not having even realised what she was doing, but Ben had given her a veiled look, his eyes gleaming with sensuality.

'I'm so sorry; I didn't know I was doing it. I must have been out of my mind,' she had whispered and he had smiled oddly.

'Don't apologise. I wanted you going crazy. I like you that way.'

He liked it now. She heard his little gasps of pleasure, but by then she was past caring about anything. The wild, compulsive rhythm was building up; their bodies were becoming one flesh, moving convulsively together, perspiration dewing their skins, the heat growing intolerable.

It was like being consumed with fire. She felt her very hair crackling with heat, her body twisting and shuddering in the flame, an agonising desire leaping up inside her, and in her arms Ben was gasping like a parched man, his long groans of pleasure so sharp, they were like cries of pain.

Afterwards they lay still in a silence that held echoes of the sounds they had just made. Nerissa came back slowly through layers of sensual experience, her body chilling, her mind even colder.

Her aunt and uncle's bedroom was just across the passage—they must have heard them, surely! The very thought of anyone else hearing her moaning out in that feverish abandonment made her feel ill.

But even worse was the knowledge that the glass dome of the past had been shattered. Ben had intended to do it, and he had succeeded. In his arms

just now she had betrayed Philip and everything he
stood for—the golden illusions of innocent
childhood, the pangs of first love, the fairy-tale
which had ended so tragically, the pain of separation which had only been comforted by a sense of
fidelity. She had betrayed it all and it would never
be the same again. The enchantment was over, the
spell broken.

She wished she were dead.

CHAPTER FOUR

NERISSA fell asleep at last, only to be woken up abruptly in the early morning by the shrill of the telephone downstairs.

Her sleep-drowned brain registered the sound as an alarm bell; she fell out of bed and only when she found herself standing up did she realise what had woken her, where she was, and then, with a stunned shock, that she was stark naked.

That was when she remembered the night before.

She saw her nightie on the floor and grabbed it up, pulled it down over her head with flustered fingers, afraid that Ben was watching her.

He wasn't, though. He wasn't in her bed any more—he had got into his own some time during the night and was stirring drowsily on his pillow, his dark hair ruffled against the white linen which her aunt had been given as a wedding present a quarter of a century ago and which she kept starched and beautifully ironed, smelling of lavender and fresh air.

He looked younger in sleep; she had never noticed that before but she did now. She stared, absorbing the change in him—his powerful face was relaxed, almost boyish, his mouth slightly open, a flush of sleep on his cheekbones.

Nerissa felt a strange qualm. She hurriedly looked away, then realised that the phone was still ringing—nobody had answered it. That was odd because at this hour her aunt and uncle were usually up. A glance at the clock told her it was just gone half-past eight.

Maybe Aunt Grace had already left for the hospital and Uncle John would be out on the farm somewhere? They must have gone quietly, allowing her and Ben to sleep undisturbed.

She got her dressing-gown from behind the door, where it hung as it always had during her childhood, shouldered into it and ran downstairs.

Whoever was ringing was being very persistent, and that bothered her. Bad news, she thought, snatching up the phone. It had to be bad news. Was Philip worse? Or even ... No! She wouldn't think about anything worse.

'Hello?'

'Hello? That isn't Mrs Thornton, is it? Is it her niece?'

'Yes, this is Nerissa Havelock.' The voice was vaguely familiar although she couldn't quite remember where she knew it from.

A smile invaded the voice. 'Oh, hello,' the other woman said warmly. 'I thought I recognised your voice! This is Staff Nurse Courtney.'

Nerissa's heart nearly stopped. After a second of grinding shock she said huskily, 'Oh, yes, hello, Staff Nurse.' Her mouth was dry; she ran her tongue-tip round her lips, almost whispered, 'Has something ... happened?'

Behind her she heard a movement on the stairs and glanced back to see her aunt standing there, in her shabby old green wool dressing-gown and new pink slippers, gripping the balustrade, her face white with fear.

Nerissa wanted to run to comfort her, but then she realised what she was being told and stayed, transfixed, her knuckles white as she gripped the phone.

'Don't sound so worried! It's not bad news!' Staff Nurse Courtney laughed excitedly, her voice lilting. 'In fact, it's the opposite. He just opened his eyes! Ten minutes ago, while I was washing his face. I was talking away to him, telling him he needed another shave again and making stupid jokes about how fast his beard grew, when suddenly his eyes opened and he looked at me, said something like, "Sorry to be such a nuisance," and I almost dropped dead on the spot!'

Nerissa leaned back against the wall to stop herself falling down. 'Oh, God,' she broke out, trembling.

Grace Thornton was beside her now. 'What? What?' she asked fiercely. 'He isn't dead? Nerissa, what is she saying?'

'He's out of the coma,' Nerissa said, crying and smiling at the same time, and held out the phone to her.

Her aunt took it, staring blindly at Nerissa. 'Out of the coma?' she repeated, as if afraid to believe it, then she gave a long, wrenched sigh. 'Oh, Nerissa!' She put the phone to her ear. 'Hello? Staff Nurse? Grace Thornton here.'

Out of the corner of her eye Nerissa saw Ben walking down the stairs towards them. He was in pyjamas, over them a maroon silk dressing-gown she had bought him for his birthday two months ago. His hair was still ruffled but the flush on his cheeks had gone—he was quite pale, in fact, she thought, frowning and doing a double-take.

He looked almost as shocked as she felt.

He must have been woken up by movements and voices; he had obviously heard what she'd said to her aunt. Their eyes met; his were hard, inimical, searching her face for clues to what she was thinking. Nerissa looked away, refusing to let him read her as if she were a book.

She wasn't even sure yet, herself, what she thought. At the moment she was simply feeling— a surge of joy because Philip had regained consciousness, gladness for Aunt Grace and Uncle John, a weak relief that the strain and anguish of the past few days had just been lifted from them all.

She walked towards the kitchen. Her blood sugar was low; she needed a quick injection of energy.

She concentrated on mundane details to try to calm herself down. Moving slowly, a little jerkily, like a robot, she filled the percolator, put it on, got out cups and saucers, plates and cereal bowls, laying the table for breakfast and seeing that someone had already been down this morning—presumably Uncle John, who must have breakfasted on cereal, since a packet of branflakes still stood on the table. He had made tea for himself—the pot was still there, cold—and there was a used cup and a cereal bowl in the washing-up machine.

Aunt Grace had obviously overslept—or had Uncle John turned off their alarm clock deliberately to let her sleep on? Nerissa wouldn't be surprised. Her aunt had looked exhausted last night.

If she hadn't slept late she would have been at the hospital now. Maybe she would have been there when her son woke up? After all those hours of watching it seemed ironic that he should come out of his coma when she wasn't there.

The thought made Nerissa sad. Aunt Grace deserved to have been there when Philip woke up. Fate was always playing these cruel tricks on people.

Ben came into the kitchen, closed the door on Aunt Grace's husky murmuring voice and leaned on it, his arms folded, watching Nerissa.

'So he's out of the coma? Do they know yet if he's suffered brain damage?'

The question jolted her; she frowned. It was on the cards, obviously. She knew they had to face that. Philip had suffered serious injuries, had been in a coma for days—would he ever be quite the same again? What if he was a human vegetable for the rest of his life?

She looked angrily at Ben. He would rain on their parade, wouldn't he? Couldn't he allow them a little space for joy?

The coffee had begun to percolate; she turned away to deal with it, said coldly over her shoulder, 'What do you want for breakfast? I could cook you something—eggs, bacon, mushrooms?'

'What are you having?'

'I haven't thought. I'm not hungry.'

'Too happy, no doubt,' he drawled, and a shiver ran down her spine at the note in his voice, but she wouldn't react, wouldn't let him see that his sharp little needles were getting under her skin.

Sometimes she almost thought he disliked her. He might want her, but there was dark hostility buried under his amused, mocking observation of her at times. Ben was a proud, hard man—self-sufficient, in control of his life. Did he resent her? Did he see it as a weakness, a flaw in his character?

Curtly, she said, 'I'll just have a poached egg, I think, but you can have whatever you like.'

He smiled crookedly. 'A poached egg on toast would be fine, thanks.'

The door opened as she was getting out the poaching-pan. Nerissa looked round at Aunt Grace, her own happiness a reflection of the joy she saw in the older woman's face.

'Isn't it wonderful news? Oh, Nerissa, I don't know what to do with myself, I'm so happy...'

Nerissa hugged her, kissed her cheek, but said, 'Before you rush off to the hospital you must have some breakfast—we're having poached eggs; do you want the same?'

'I'm not hungry, Nerissa! I couldn't eat a thing.' But Grace inhaled the fragrance in the room. 'Mmm...coffee...just what I need.'

Nerissa pushed her down on to a chair by the kitchen table, poured her a cup of coffee. 'You sit there and drink that while I deal with these eggs. Breakfast won't be five minutes. You'll be ill if you don't eat anything.'

'I'll make the toast,' said Ben, getting orange juice from the fridge and handing it to Grace Thornton. 'This will help, too. Natural sugar for your blood.'

She took it, smiled blissfully at him, then said, eyes widening, 'John! I must let him know. He'd never forgive me if I didn't. I wonder where he's working this morning? I think he said something about finishing off the walls in Great Meadow, then moving the sheep from Top Fields in there.'

'After breakfast I'll walk up there and give him the news,' Ben offered.

'Oh, thanks, lad,' Grace said gratefully. 'It's quite a climb, mind! Sure you're up to it?'

'I think I'll manage,' Ben said with a dry intonation.

Grace gave him a thoughtful look. 'Aye, of course. Well, best not wear one of your good suits or it'll be ruined. Did you pack anything more casual?'

Ben was smilingly indulgent of her concern. 'I'll wear jeans and a sweater, don't worry!'

The breakfast was ready. They all sat down and ate two eggs each with buttered toast. Afterwards, Nerissa firmly told Grace that she would clear the table and sent her aunt upstairs to have a bath and get ready to go to the hospital.

Ben helped load the dishwasher. Coolly, he said, 'When we've got dressed you can show me the way to this place where your uncle is working.'

'I'll draw you a map—you'll find it easily enough,' Nerissa told him. 'I'll go to the hospital with Aunt Grace.'

'You won't!' Ben said, and the lash of his voice made her start, look round at him in shock.

'Don't give me orders! I'm going with my aunt and you aren't stopping me!'

'She doesn't want you there!' Ben bit out and Nerissa froze, staring at him. His face was cool, his grey eyes level, hard. 'She's his mother. She's been living in a nightmare ever since he had that accident—give her a little while alone with him, for God's sake.'

Nerissa bit her lip, realising he was right, hating him for being right.

She turned away without a word, pressed the button that started the dishwasher, threw a look around the once more immaculate kitchen, then made for the stairs.

Aunt Grace was out of the bathroom. Nerissa collected some clothes and went in to wash and get dressed.

When she returned to the bedroom Ben was standing by the window staring out; he looked round, his eyes flicking down over her. She had put on an old pair of jodhpurs which she had left behind here when she'd gone to London but which still fitted her like a glove. With them she wore a polo-necked yellow sweater which she had also had for years—it was slightly too tight but she had always worn it with her jodhpurs so she had put it on.

'I haven't seen that gear before,' he drawled, his gaze fixed on the warm swell of her breasts under the close-fitting sweater.

'These are old clothes I haven't worn for years. The bathroom's yours,' she said shortly, angrily conscious of heat in her face at the way he was staring.

Ben noticed her flush—his faintly derisive glance told her so—but he didn't say anything, simply went out to the bathroom.

Nerissa tidied the bedroom and made their beds. She had almost finished when her aunt appeared wearing one of her best dresses—a soft pink jersey wool she rarely wore except on very special occasions.

'You look lovely!' said Nerissa spontaneously and Grace Thornton smiled, her face radiant.

'Thanks love. Are you ready?'

Nerissa smiled, shaking her head. 'You go, Aunt Grace. I'll see him later. I think I'd better show Ben the way up to Great Meadow to find Uncle John or he might get lost.'

She knew Ben had been right when her aunt's face altered just a fraction—there was a brightening of her eyes, a lifting of her smile.

'OK, dear. See you later, then.'

Nerissa watched her aunt hurry away, feeling guilty. She wanted to see Philip, she was aching to see him, to find out what his accident, the brain surgery, the long coma had done to him, but this moment belonged to his mother. I should have thought of it, she angrily admitted. I should have known how she would feel. I did know, of course I did, I just ... didn't think! It made her feel worse that it should have been Ben who'd pointed it out, made her realise how thoughtless she was being.

Ben walked back into the room, fully dressed too now in pale blue jeans and a dark tan sweater. His black hair was still damp, his skin freshly shaved. She felt her pulses leap at the sight of him and was angry with herself for that instant reaction.

'Ready?' he asked and she nodded.

The autumn morning was perfect, the sun mellow and warm on their backs as they walked, the sky a vivid blue, the trees shedding their leaves in a golden rain, the heather still purple on the moors, the bracken turning russet. A sparrowhawk hovered on a warm spiral of air in the distance, but it was their passing that made rabbits freeze then dart for cover, white scuts showing as they dived down their burrows.

'Uphill all the way, I'm afraid,' Nerissa told Ben drily.

'In this weather it's a pleasure, though. You can see for miles this morning, can't you?'

'From Great Meadow you get a wonderful view of Hadrian's Wall.'

'I'd like to walk the wall one day, from one end to the other,' Ben said, climbing a stile in a dry-stone wall. He stiffened, watching as a fox shot across the field in front of them, a flash of tawny orange, almost silent, moving so fast that it was out of sight behind a belt of trees in seconds.

'Does your uncle hunt?' Ben asked and Nerissa shook her head.

'No, he did when he was young, but not any more. There are a lot of foxes around—they take hens now and then, but he tries to make the runs fox-proof and you have to learn to live with the occasional loss.'

'I suppose he loses stock from natural causes anyway?'

She nodded. 'Sheep, particularly, seem to be prone to any number of diseases. They're stupid, too. They are always clambering up walls and falling off, breaking a leg or their neck, or eating something that they shouldn't. The problem of foxes is nothing compared to what the sheep get up to all by themselves! A fox won't go for a fully grown sheep anyway, but you sometimes find a vixen with young to feed will attack new-born lambs. Their

instinct is to go for weak ones, and that does annoy
Uncle John. But nature is cruel, you know; you
should see what foxes do to a hen-run if they get
into it!'

'Yes, I've heard they go crazy.'

She paused, breathing fast; it was months since
she had made this climb and she was out of
condition.

'Sit down before you have a heart attack!' Ben
said drily, watching her flushed face. He threw
himself down on a rough tussock of heathery grass
and Nerissa sat down too.

'But animals only kill for food, don't they?
Which is more than you can say about our own
species,' Ben said.

'Watch a cat playing with a mouse when it isn't
even hungry,' Nerissa said. 'It's their instinct to kill,
hungry or not.'

'Instincts are dangerous things,' Ben agreed,
looking through his lashes at her.

She ignored the personal note in his voice. 'A fox
will kill every hen in a run and leave the place lit-
tered with dead bodies,' she said bleakly. 'They get
excited by the smell of blood—once they start
killing they can't stop. Hawks, now—they only kill
for food and they mostly live on rabbits, mice and
rats, and that's more a help than a problem on a
farm. The fewer rats around, the better farmers like
it! That's why we keep a lot of wild cats in the
barns; you'll notice them if——'

She broke off as barking startled them both.

'Jess,' realised Nerissa, getting to her feet.

'Who?' Ben got up too and they began to climb
upwards again.

'One of the sheepdogs—the old one. Uncle John always has her with him, wherever he goes. She's his favourite dog.'

'How many does he have?'

'At the moment, three. Jess is the mother of the other two. Uncle John kept one out of each litter she had. He only let her whelp twice because she's a working dog, not a breeding dog. He kept a young bitch called Sally, which he thought took after Jess, and then there's Rocket, who's a couple of years older. Uncle John kept him because he was the best-looking of Jess's first litter. They're both good working dogs but Jess is still his favourite; she has forgotten more about working sheep than the other two have learnt yet.'

Behind Jess John Thornton loomed, staring down at them, and Nerissa waved, beckoning to him.

He came at a run with Jess loping in front of him, barking, showing her teeth at the strange man beside Nerissa.

'Down, Jess!' John Thornton shouted.

The sheepdog dropped to the ground beside Nerissa, flattered herself, tail wagging, her tongue lolling out, looking up obsequiously at her master as he arrived.

'What's happened?' John Thornton broke out, his face drawn and pale.

Nerissa hurriedly reassured him. 'He's out of the coma, and talking!'

John Thornton let out a long sigh. 'Thank God. Did they tell you . . . is he going to be OK? I mean, does he seem . . . is the damage bad or . . . can't they tell yet?'

'Too early to tell, but Staff Nurse Courtney said he talked quite rationally to her, and she has experience of cases like this. I think she would spot it if there was anything very wrong.'

John Thornton sighed again. 'You've told Grace? I left her in bed, asleep, I thought she needed the rest. Did you...?'

'She knows; she has already gone to the hospital. She couldn't wait to get there, but she asked us to find you and let you know.'

'She must be over the moon,' John Thornton said, smiling crookedly. 'Well, I'll have to wash and change out of my working clothes first. I can't go like this. Are you two coming in with me, or driving there in Ben's car?' He snapped his fingers at his dog and Jess was up at once, her eyes fixed adoringly on him.

Nerissa opened her mouth to say she would go with him but Ben beat her to it.

'We won't come just yet. You go on ahead—we'll see him later today.'

She gave him a furious look. He was making a habit of interfering in her life; she was sick of it.

'Sure?' John Thornton said, looking from one to the other, his expression uncertain.

'Quite sure. You and your wife will want some time alone with him at first, it's only natural. We realise that, don't we, Nerissa?' said Ben coolly. 'And I imagine the hospital wouldn't approve of his having too many visitors, not at this stage. I expect they'll want to make a lot of tests as soon as possible, to make sure he's OK. So you go on— we'll come along this afternoon.'

His fingers curled around Nerissa's arm, tightened like an iron bracelet, a silent imperative, ordering her to agree. She felt his eyes issue the same demand but didn't look at him, still resenting him, even though what he had said made sense.

Her eyes stayed on the older man; she smiled. 'We'll come along later. Give him my love, say I'll see him soon and I'm glad...so glad he's awake...'

John Thornton's face was full of confused, muddled emotion—joy mingled with sadness, guilt with pity.

'My dear——' he began and she had to stop him, cut him off, with Ben there, listening, watching them both.

'You'd better hurry. Aunt Grace will be wondering where you've got to!'

John Thornton bent and kissed her cheek. 'See you both this afternoon, then.'

He strode off down the tussocky grass with the black and white sheepdog running ahead of him. Nerissa watched him go with a choked feeling in her throat.

When he was out of earshot, to help her deal with her own pain she turned on Ben, her blue eyes blazing.

'Don't you ever do that again!'

'Do what?' he returned blandly, but watching her like one of the hawks that haunted these hills—narrow-eyed and lethal in the blue sky, watching a mouse in the grass below.

'You know what I'm talking about! Stop interfering in my life!'

'You were going to charge off to the hospital; I had to stop you. It was obvious that it never oc-

curred to you that you might be in the way, that
the Thorntons might want to be alone with their
son, just at first.' Ben's voice was coolly contemptuous and brought an angry flush to her face.

'You seem to forget I've been part of their family
most of my life! I'm not some stranger who's
barging in on a private moment. I grew up with
Philip and I know they would want me to be there—
after all, they rang me to ask me to come up here.
So will you just leave me alone and stay out of my
way? Go back to London. I don't want you here.'

'I'm sure you don't. Now that your beloved
Philip is back in the land of the living you want to
spend every possible moment alone with him, of
course.'

The drawling sarcasm made her hand screw up
at her sides as she fought a strong desire to hit him.
He glanced down at those tell-tale hands, his brows
lifting.

'Lost for words, Nerissa? You don't deny it, I
notice.' He gave her a mocking smile that made her
temper shoot up.

'Why should I bother?' she muttered back. 'You
apparently know more about me than I do—why
should I waste my time contradicting you?'

He bared his teeth at her in angry amusement.
'Then I hope you won't contradict me when I tell
you that not only am I staying on until the weekend,
but when I go back to London on Sunday night
you are coming with me.'

She drew a fierce breath, shaking her head, her
black hair blowing in the moorland wind, wild as
the mane of one of the hill ponies that roamed the
more secret parts of this district, their shaggy, un-

kempt coats keeping them warm in the coldest weather.

'I won't!' she insisted.

'You will, Nerissa!' He wasn't smiling now. His face was hard, remote, as if she were a stranger he disliked—and perhaps she was?

He thought he knew her so well, and yet she was certain he hardly knew her at all. What he did know he didn't like.

She had seen that look on his face before, in court, when he was cross-examining a hostile witness, the icy rapier of his wit and his stinging sarcasm giving short shrift to anyone foolish enough to try to snap back at him. She should have remembered that Ben would use any weapon to win a case; winning was what mattered to him, in his career and in his life.

She was his wife. Ben thought of her as one of his possessions—he had even admitted it, hadn't he? He had said that he still wanted her body, and while he did he was not ready to let her go.

A shiver ran down her back. She was so disturbed that she felt she had to get away from him. She would go for a long walk across the moors alone, give herself a chance to think.

She turned and started to walk away without another word, unable, in fact, to say anything to him.

'Where do you think you're going?' Ben demanded, catching her by the arm and holding her back.

She glared up at him. 'I need to think. I'm going for a walk.'

'Not alone you're not.' He glanced up at the desolate, empty hills, his brows meeting. 'Are you crazy? There isn't a living soul in sight for miles. If anything happened to you it could be hours before anyone found you.'

'I know these hills like the back of my hand. Philip and I used to spend all day up there.' She stared at the horizon, her eyes clouding over as she remembered. It had been the happiest time of her life—growing up, falling in love, knowing she was loved in return. Dreamily, she said aloud, to herself, rather than Ben, 'We used to take a picnic, wander around, pick blueberries in the summer among the heather, get our legs and hands scratched without minding and then lie down in the long grass to eat the berries, to hear the bees humming around the clover or watch grasshoppers jumping—you know, if you catch one and hold it cupped between your palms it hops around, trying to escape. It's the weirdest feeling, so you open your hands and it sails out.'

She was so rapt that she forgot who she was talking to until he suddenly interrupted.

'For God's sake! It's over. You can't go back; that door is shut for you forever. Stop living in the past!'

She looked up at him then, brought back to the present, to Ben, to the bitter realisation that for that moment she had been living in a time long gone and golden with happiness, and now Ben had deliberately dragged her back.

He watched her changing expression, the darkening of her eyes, the paling of her skin, and his own face tightened.

'Maybe I like the past better,' she threw back at him, her voice husky and quivering with pain and regrets.

'My God, sometimes I swear I could hit you,' he ground out through his teeth and, as if to emphasise that, caught hold of her shoulders and shook her, her head going backwards, flopping and limp, like a rag doll's.

'Stop it! What do you think you're doing? Let go of me, damn you!' Nerissa attempted to struggle out of his grip only to find herself being jerked towards him, the hard male body pressing into her, forcing her to be aware of his desire.

She shuddered at the contact. 'Don't!'

The rejection was like petrol flung on a bonfire; Ben blazed up, his grey eyes white-hot, his mouth a bitter line.

'I'm tired of living with the memory of another man coming between us all the time! What can I do to get him out of your head, Nerissa? You can never have him. When are you going to face up to that?'

He caught hold of her hair with one hand, tugged on it to tilt her head back, and then his mouth relentlessly came down on hers in a kiss which held no tenderness or even passion; the heat in it was all anger.

Rage shot up inside her, too, as if to match his— gushed out of her like raw black oil out of the ground, darkening the sky of her mind.

She was angry because she knew why he was kissing her with that punishing violence. It had jarred Ben's pride when she'd rejected him just now.

That was the only reason why he was so angry. He didn't love her; he merely felt he owned her. She was his wife, she had no business saying no to him if he wanted her.

Nerissa's life had been ruined by stupid pride once before. She wasn't going to let it happen again.

She hit out wildly. Ben instinctively jerked back from her slap and fell, but as he went down he grabbed for her and took her with him, their bodies tangling, colliding.

They landed heavily. All the breath was knocked out of Nerissa and she couldn't think for a second as she found herself on her back, looking up at the blue sky.

Then Ben was on top of her, his head blocking out the sky, his face taut and darkly flushed, his eyes glittering with an urgency that made her heart thud into her ribcage, her mouth go dry with fear.

Her throat had closed up, she was trembling violently, she couldn't get a word out.

She shook her head, tried to push him away, her hands splayed against his shoulders, her body arching in protest.

He kissed her again, harder, forcing her head back into the thick, tussocky grass and heather which scratched the back of her neck quite painfully although she was only vaguely aware of it.

Ben's hand moved possessively and she shuddered as she felt his fingers caress the warm swell of her breast in the tight yellow sweater, then the hand moved on, pushed her sweater upwards; he pushed his knee between her legs and parted them, slid between them.

He wasn't just going to kiss her. With a stab of real horror she realised that he was going to force her to have sex with him, here and now, whether she wanted it or not.

'Not here,' she muttered, twisting and turning underneath him. 'For God's sake, Ben, not here...'

He lifted his head to look down at her, a harshness in his voice. 'Yes, here, Nerissa! Next time you think about this hillside, you won't be thinking about being here with him—you're going to remember being up here with me.'

CHAPTER FIVE

NERISSA looked at Ben with a shiver of dismay. He was taking all her memories and wrecking them one by one; he had begun last night, making love to her with that almost barbaric insistence in the house, under the same roof where she and Philip had grown up together, fallen in love. Now he was going to make love to her with the same brutal demand up here on the hillside where she and Philip had walked, run, lain in the sun and talked and laughed together.

'Why are you doing this?' she burst out, and saw Ben's eyes flicker as if in wariness or uncertainty, as if he wasn't quite sure himself why he was ruthlessly setting out to ruin her memories of the past.

But he answered, his voice harsh. 'When you agreed to marry me you said you were going to forget him; you said you wanted to forget him...'

'That's not true! I could never forget Philip—how could I? I might as well say I wanted to forget myself. I told you the past was over and it is, but Philip is me—a large part of me anyway, just as I'm part of him and always will be.'

'As brother and sister,' Ben said through tight lips. 'You grew up that close. As near as dammit you grew up as brother and sister. You should never have dreamt of becoming lovers. And God knows you can never be lovers again.'

'I know that!' she muttered angrily. 'We both know that! But how could I possibly forget him? What am I supposed to do—have a lobotomy to remove my memory? Block out my entire life? Never come back here again? They are my family, this is my old home—I'd lose too much. And even if I'd meant to stay away, all that changed when Philip had this terrible accident. I had to come back then. They needed me; they hoped I could get through to him—why else did they ring me? They thought he might come back—for me...' Her voice broke and she swallowed, heard Ben's harsh intake of breath.

'That's something else I don't understand—how they could ask you to do it? After what they'd done to you. I'd have thought that they would have more of a sense of decency. Oh, your aunt, I can forgive her—I have a lot of respect for her and he is her only son—but his father...'

'Don't talk about him. You have no right to take that tone every time you mention him. Aunt Grace is the only one who has a right to despise him...'

'What about you? My God, Nerissa—in your place I'd have nothing but contempt for the man!'

He didn't need to tell her that—she could see it in his eyes, in his cold face, the look of distaste, and she knew John Thornton had seen the same expression in the past. Ben had the ability to convey what he thought and felt without saying a word. It was an inestimable gift in a courtroom; he could devastate silently, reduce a witness to a quivering wreck with a lift of those fine black brows.

'You aren't me,' she muttered. Looking back, she remembered how she had felt once, in the beginning—the pain and shock and horror of discovering that John Thornton was not the saintly, perfect human being she had always thought him. It had taken a while for her to get over finding out that he had feet of clay, was capable of doing things Nerissa still couldn't bear to think about. She hadn't understood why he had done it and for some months she had hated him, but her love was stronger, had deeper roots, and she had gone over it again and again in her mind and slowly realised that although everything had changed some things would always remain the same. She loved Uncle John, and Aunt Grace—they were the only parents she could ever remember and they had given her unfailing love all through her childhood.

'You expect too much of people,' she told Ben. 'You're too unforgiving.'

He had never forgiven his first wife. Nerissa had often felt curious about Aileen, who had married her lover after Ben divorced her. She had never actually met the other woman. Aileen and her husband had gone to live in Japan where he was working for an oil company; Aileen had had two children by him, apparently. Nerissa wondered about that too—how had Ben felt when he'd heard that news?

Ben kept no photographs of his first wife around, but Nerissa knew that Aileen had been fair, with a kittenish face and slanting green eyes, because she had seen a picture of them both in Ben's family home. His mother was dead, and his rather frail seventy-year-old father lived with his married daughter Jenny, her husband Jack and their three children. They had all moved into the old man's home to look after him; they would, in any case, inherit the house since Ben had agreed to waive any claim to it. He had a very high income; his brother-in-law was a teacher who earned nowhere near as much—it seemed to Ben a fair division, especially as his sister was taking care of their father and had given up a lot of her time to nursing their mother before she died.

Nerissa had hoped that she and Jenny would become friends, but when they'd first met she'd soon realised that Jenny wasn't willing to like her.

Jenny had been at school with Aileen; they had remained friends, and wrote to each other all the time, even now that Aileen lived in Japan. But it was hardly Nerissa's fault that Ben's marriage had broken up. He had been divorced for six years before he even met her.

Nevertheless, Jenny Lister had been unfriendly when they'd met, and Ben's father had not seemed quite sure who Nerissa was—he'd kept calling her Aileen and asking her why she had dyed her hair black; he preferred it fair. His memory was failing; he missed his wife and had lost interest in life.

'It wouldn't do you any harm to toughen up,' said Ben now. 'Shut the door on yesterday, Nerissa. All this backward-looking doesn't do you any good.'

'You can't turn off love like a tap,' she said sadly.

'Ah, we're back to Philip again, are we? I'm sick of hearing his name, do you know that? Shut up about him. Just stop talking about him, thinking about him.' He framed her face with his hands and their eyes met and held. Ben's stare had the glitter of dark stars, and Nerissa felt her heart begin to beat fast.

'I'm going to get him out of your head if it's the last thing I do,' Ben muttered, and began to kiss her again, not with the same angry brutality, but slowly, deeply, with hot sensuality.

Her body always betrayed her when he touched her like that; it reacted now, immediately, with the usual quivering sensitivity towards him, swinging like a compass needle to the magnetic north, helpless against the law of its own nature.

Eyes closed, she shut out the sunlight and the blue sky; darkness overtook her and she arched, moaning, wanting him fiercely. All the emotional turmoil of the last few days needed this release, the discharge of all that frustrated energy. Ben achieved what he wanted; he managed to make her forget everything but what he was doing to her.

Until they were interrupted.

Ben was the first to realise they were no longer alone. He stiffened suddenly, breaking off that long, passionate kiss, lifting his head, grunting, 'What the hell...?'

Nerissa was just opening her eyes when she felt a tongue licking her face. A warm, wet tongue. And with it came the sound of something sniffing at her, a nose questing among her long, curling clouds of black hair.

Her blue eyes opened wide; she saw a silky dark red head, big melting brown eyes, an open mouth full of teeth, a mouth which panted happily, grinning at her.

Nerissa began to laugh wildly. 'My God, I wondered what it was! Where have you come from, you bad dog?'

Ben had rolled off her by then and was sitting up, eyeing the animal with disfavour.

'Is it one of the farm dogs?'

'No, it's from the pub in the village.' Nerissa grabbed the dog by its long, silky coat of hair, then saw the lead trailing from its collar and caught hold of that. 'It must have run off while Job was taking it for a walk! Didn't you meet Job Nicholson when you came up here? He's the landlord—big man with grey hair, doesn't talk much but his wife, Sylvia, more than makes up for it? This is his dog; he dotes on the silly animal.'

'Heaven knows why!' Ben grunted, watching the dog flopping beside Nerissa with a long, gusty sigh. 'Does it often come up to visit the farm?'

'If it can get away it does, unfortunately. Job keeps it on the lead when he takes it out—the village policeman warned him what would happen if he didn't. This silly thing chases sheep. Doesn't attack them, just runs around barking, scaring the daylights out of them. A couple of years ago a ewe in lamb broke a leg running away from him in panic and Uncle John said he'd shoot it if he saw it chasing his sheep again. Job Nicholson will be frantic if he thinks it has come up here. We had better take it down to the farm and ring Job.'

'If I had a gun with me I'd shoot it myself,' muttered Ben, scowling at the grinning dog.

'Don't you like dogs?' she asked, tongue-in-cheek, shooting a sideways look at him through her lowered lashes.

His answering glance was smouldering. 'Don't be provocative, Nerissa! You know why I could kill that stupid animal. He came along just at the wrong moment.'

For Ben, maybe. Not for her, thought Nerissa. If the dog hadn't arrived when it did she would have let Ben make love to her, and she would be regretting it bitterly by now, all her memories of herself and Philip up here on these hills obliterated by something very different.

Ben was quite a psychologist.

She wished she were—wished she understood her husband a little better; he baffled her at times— she couldn't be certain of his motivation. Pride didn't seem a good enough reason for the anger he kept showing. She looked down at the dog, whose long ears she was fondling, and grimaced to herself. Pride could make people do some very odd things. She knew that—none better. Her whole life had been ruined by other people's pride.

'Do you think it has been chasing sheep this morning? Should we go and check on the flock up here?' asked Ben and she shook her head.

'Believe me, we'd have heard it. Not just the dog barking but the sheep—they make a hell of a racket when they're frightened. I expect he was on his way to Great Meadow, until he was distracted by seeing us.'

She got to her feet, still holding on to the red setter. 'That will teach you to be curious,' she told him indulgently, and the dog looked up at her, pleased with itself, grinning. 'But you're a lovely boy, aren't you?' she added, ruffling his coat again. 'Come on, dog.' She made a face at Ben. 'I can't

call him by his name—I can't remember what Job
calls him.'

'I could suggest something!' Ben said drily and
she laughed, setting off down the hill with Ben
coming more slowly behind her.

They got back to the farm in half the time it had
taken them to climb up. Nerissa had to yank on the
lead to stop the red setter from pulling her arm out;
he set quite a pace, loping ahead on his long,
graceful legs, his tongue lolling out in excitement.
By the time they reached the farm she was out of
breath and her arm ached.

'Why don't we take the dog back to this pub and
eat there?' suggested Ben as she reached for the
phone to ring Job Nicholson. 'They do bar lunches
every day, don't they?'

'Very good ones,' agreed Nerissa, dialling. 'Fine.
What time is it? Eleven-thirty already! What time
shall we go? I want to get to the hospital early in
the afternoon.'

'I'm hungry now, after all that exercise,' Ben
said, adding softly with a mocking undertone, 'And
all that emotion.'

She pretended not to hear that. 'I'll tell Job to
expect us in half an hour, then, OK?'

Job was pathetically grateful. 'Thanks for letting
me know, love. I've been having nightmares, wondering if your uncle would catch him chasing sheep
and shoot him! I even rang to ask if he had been
spotted up there, but there was no reply.'

'They're at the hospital and I was out on the
farm,' explained Nerissa. 'That's how I ran into
him. He was galloping about all over the hill but I

don't think he had met up with the sheep yet, so there's no harm done. How did he get away?'

'I was out in the village and met Sam Nidd; we were stood there chatting and the damn animal suddenly took off like a rocket. I couldn't catch him. I drove around in the car looking for him, but he was nowhere to be seen, crafty little beggar. I'll come up and get him now, love.'

'There's no need, Job. We're coming down to eat a bar lunch in a little while; we'll bring him with us.'

'Then you must have it on me! I owe you a good lunch for doing me such a big favour.'

'There's no need...' she began, but Job said gruffly,

'I insist! And thanks, love. Believe me, if anything happened to that dog I'd be a bear with a sore head for weeks.'

She smiled. 'I know. OK, Job, see you later.'

She went into the kitchen to catch Ben giving the red setter a bowl of water which it lapped eagerly.

He looked round as she entered, said sheepishly, 'He seemed thirsty. I could do with a drink myself, actually.'

'Help yourself,' she said. 'I'm going to change my clothes; I won't be long.'

He stared at her broodingly. 'Going to make yourself look beautiful for Philip?'

She ignored that, turned on her heel and walked out. Upstairs she took off her jodhpurs and put on a long black skirt, changed her yellow sweater for a flowing white shirt with a frilled jabot collar and added a black and white striped waistcoat, its formality in provocative contrast to the soft femi-

ninity of her shirt. She brushed her long black curls
and did her make-up—made her generous mouth
a hot red, stroked dark blue shadow on to her lids,
darkened her long lashes, dusted her skin with light
powder.

The mirror told her she looked terrific; when she
got back downstairs Ben's eyes were more explicit.

'So!' he said in a soft, angry explosion.

'So what?' she asked, lifting one graceful,
darkened brow.

He had been drinking; there was a glass of whisky
and soda water in his hand, the ice clinking as he
put the drink down on a table with a bang. She
hoped he hadn't had more than one. He was going
to be driving. Maybe she should suggest that she
drive the car? Yet she hesitated to do that. There
was an angry glitter in his eyes that worried her. It
was unusual for Ben to drink; he was normally a
very abstemious, disciplined man.

'You realise you're playing with fire, don't you?'
he muttered, his eyes skimming down over her lin-
geringly. 'If you go to see him looking like that
you'll send his temperature sky-high. Why don't
you let the poor devil alone?'

She caught her breath, wounded. 'What is that
supposed to mean? I haven't even been up here for
months, you know that, and the last time I came
you were with me!'

'But you haven't let him go, have you?' Ben said
in a scathing voice. 'You still have him on the end
of a line and you know it. Why else did his parents
send for you when they realised how serious his
injuries were? You admitted it yourself—they hoped
he'd react to your voice, even if he didn't react to

theirs! They were under no illusions. They knew he hadn't forgotten you, any more than you have forgotten him!'

'How could we—either of us?' she whispered, chalk-white, her eyes like bruised blue flowers in her shadowy face. Fate had cheated them of the fulfilment of their love but it couldn't kill it; it had roots which went too deep.

Ben caught hold of her slender shoulders and shook her angrily. 'You have to, Nerissa! Stop living in a fool's paradise. You can't have him and it is killing you... both of you... to go on like this. Hasn't it occurred to you to wonder about this accident he had? I talked to his father about it yesterday; the police said the accident was baffling— it shouldn't have happened; he hadn't been drunk and there was nothing wrong with his car. He simply seems to have driven like a madman, almost hit another car, crashed straight into a stone wall. They talked to his parents, trying to find out why he should have been driving like that. Had he had a row with someone? Was something worrying him? they asked them, but of course his parents told them no.'

'They would,' she said dully.

'Their pride again,' Ben supplied and she gave a sigh, wrenched by it physically, her slight body swaying between his compelling hands.

'Their pride,' she agreed. 'They hate the idea of being gossiped about, people knowing... They would rather be pulled apart by wild horses than tell a living soul.'

'And so they drove you away to London, and drove their only son into a suicide attempt!'

It was like being punched in the stomach. Nerissa gasped in pain, in shock, staring up at him.

'No! You can't say that! There's no evidence ...'

'He'd make sure of that. He wouldn't want anyone gossiping about his death—his precious family pride has to be protected, doesn't it?'

She bit her lip so hard that blood spurted, scarcely showing on the glossy dark red of her lipstick.

Ben saw it, though. He let go of her shoulders and bent, licked her torn lip gently with the tip of his tongue.

She shivered at the brief contact. She couldn't believe he had done that! It had a strange effect on her, that perverse, disturbing little gesture. Her pulses leapt; she felt chilled and yet feverish. Not for the first time she speculated about the darkness inside Ben. He was a compulsive personality, of course, possessed by an inner drive that forced him to repeat patterns of response, behaviour, desire.

That was what made him such a brilliant lawyer. He could dazzle in court, strip people to their very bones, and yet he was also a methodical and precise man, working until all hours on the incredible amounts of paperwork his job demanded—reading briefs, looking up case law, making sheaves of notes in his small, neat, careful handwriting. He wouldn't stop searching until he had found what he was looking for.

Ben was obsessive. Wasn't that why he was reacting with such violence over Philip? He was repeating with her his rage when he'd found his wife in bed with his best friend.

She remembered his words when he'd first told her about it. 'It's a music-hall joke, isn't it? It's always the husband's best friend in these triangles—the one he trusted. I've often wondered who made the first move—Aileen or him. It's usually the guy who makes the first move, of course.'

His pride made it hard for him to accept that it might have been his wife who began that affair, Nerissa had thought at the time.

She wouldn't have been surprised to be told that it had been Aileen. There had been something in the other woman's face, even in that wedding photo—a greediness in the eyes, a cat-like self-indulgence about the mouth. Aileen had looked like the sort of woman who would get bored with the routine of marriage and look around for something else to amuse her.

All the same she had tried to be fair. 'Maybe they couldn't help themselves,' she had quietly suggested, and had seen Ben's face tighten.

'People always have a choice,' he'd snapped. 'I don't buy that stuff about being helpless. They knew the difference between right and wrong.'

'It isn't always that clear-cut!' she had protested.

'It was for them,' Ben had bit out. 'She was my wife. He was supposed to be my friend.'

'But... if they fell in love...?'

He had looked at her icily. 'Don't make excuses for them! You didn't even know them.' His eyes had been hard, cold, incisive.

They wore that expression now. He talked about her family in exactly the same way.

'Philip's their son,' he said. 'He's inherited their pride, or been taught to put it above everything else. So when he couldn't bear life any more he just walked out of this house one day and tried to kill himself in a way that wouldn't cause any scandal or inconvenience to them.'

'It was an accident!'

His shrug was scornful, dismissive. 'I don't believe in that sort of accident. Not when it gets someone out of a situation they find intolerable. Oh, I don't say he thought it all out and then cold-bloodedly went out to do it, but he was living in some sort of hell and he couldn't stand it any more. He went out and drove like a madman until he crashed. If that is what you call an accident, then OK, he had an accident. I prefer to name it more truthfully... suicide.'

She caught his arm, looked pleadingly into his face. 'Don't say anything like this to them, to his parents. Please, Ben, don't even hint at it. It would destroy them.'

'Oh, don't worry, I won't,' he muttered, scowling down at her pale fingers on his sleeve. He looked at his watch. 'We'd better be going, hadn't we?'

She looked at the time too, blankly, her mind still possessed by fear of Ben talking like that to Philip's parents. If they thought for an instant that Philip might have wanted to die... She winced at the idea of what that would do to them—particularly to his father, whose eyes were always shadowed by guilt and regret.

'Are you coming or not?' Ben ground out and she nodded.

'Yes, of course.'

They put the red setter into the back of Ben's car and drove off five minutes later. It was still sunny outside but there was a wind getting up now— golden leaves were whirling off the trees in an unceasing rain, horse-chestnuts gleamed in the grass where they had fallen and there was a scent of bonfires in the air as they drove through the village. As they got out of the car the wind briskly blew Nerissa's hair across her face and whipped her skirt up.

'It's getting cold now,' she said, hurrying inside the old, stone-built public house. Above the door swung the inn sign, hand-painted, of a man's eyes peering through a mask of green leaves. There had been a Green Man inn standing here for centuries, but then there were hundreds of Green Man inns in England; it was possibly the most common inn name. As a child Nerissa had often stared up at the sign wondering what it meant. Why was the man hiding behind leaves? Or were the leaves growing all over him? There had been something sinister about the sign to her, as a child.

Only when she grew up did she find out that the Green Man was an unforgotten piece of English history harking back to pagan times, to the old religion of the countryside, the gods who were believed to inhabit trees, rivers, animals. In some parts of the country men still dressed up in leaves and branches, or wore antlers on their heads, and went through some sort of ritual on one day a year. Old habits die hard and so do old beliefs and old loves, thought Nerissa bleakly as she preceded Ben into the comfortable bar.

They delivered the dog to his grateful owner, who rubbed his silky head fiercely, muttering to him, 'What did you do it for, you daft animal? You could have been shot, do you realise that? Of course you don't! You're too stupid.'

The dog grinned, panting, butting his owner with his head.

'Oh, aye, you think you're so clever, don't you?' The landlord took the lead and handed it to his wife who was watching with pursed lips. 'Put him in the kitchen, love, would you?'

'Next time I hope they will shoot him!' she said, marching off, pulling the dog after her as it fought to stay with its master. 'Come on, will you, you flea hotel?' she snapped at it.

Nerissa and Ben settled in a corner by a window overlooking a wind-blown garden and ate the special of the day—roast beef and Yorkshire pudding, roast potatoes, carrots, cabbage and peas. A traditional English meal, perfectly cooked.

They didn't talk much. Nerissa was on edge with excitement and nerves and Ben was in one of his curt, angry moods. She wanted to ask him to let her visit Philip alone, but she dared not—she knew he would refuse, and how he would look at her when he did.

When they got to the hospital they found Grace Thornton in the waiting-room drinking coffee from a plastic cup and eating a packet of ready-made sandwiches. She looked ten times happier than she had since the accident. Her eyes were brighter, her face had more colour, she smiled more readily.

'I came out to let the doctor visit him,' she explained. 'John has gone home again. He has a hundred jobs to do and now Philip's out of the coma he feels he must get on with things. I shan't stay all day, either; they tell me Philip will need lots of rest. I shall pop in for a little while when I've finished my sandwiches, then I'll go home and let him get some sleep.'

'Does he seem OK?' Nerissa asked nervously and her aunt nodded happily.

'As far as I can tell he's perfectly normal, but until they've seen the X-rays and brain scans and done all the tests they say they have to do they can't be certain what is happening inside his brain. So far, so good, though——' She broke off, looking towards the ward doors. 'Oh, there's the doctor leaving now—why don't you go in, Nerissa? I'll be along in five minutes.'

Her mouth dry, her nerves jumping, Nerissa walked towards the door, very conscious of Ben stalking beside her, his hard eyes on her averted profile.

Philip was alone when they pushed open the door. He was awake, lying back against the pillows, not looking their way, quietly staring out of the window, but his head turned as the door opened. He looked across the room, his face empty and still for a second, then, like a light coming on in a dark room, his face lit up.

He didn't even say her name—just held out his hand.

She stumbled to the bed and sat on the chair beside it, took his hand between both of hers, stroking it, smiling into his eyes.

They didn't need to say anything. They had always been able to read each other's mind.

Ben stood behind her, brooding, watching them both. Philip hadn't acknowledged his presence yet; it was another minute before he took his eyes off Nerissa and looked at Ben, nodded to him.

'Hello.'

'How are you?' Ben asked curtly, unsmiling.

'Not so bad.' Philip didn't pretend to be friendly; neither did Ben.

'What did the doctor say?' Nerissa asked and Philip's eyes came back to her quickly.

'He didn't say anything—they're very cagey. I have to start doing a lot of tests tomorrow. Today I'm to rest.'

'We won't stay long.'

His fingers tightened on hers. 'Don't go yet.'

They had spent most of their lives together on that isolated farm; they thought alike, they even looked alike in some ways, although Philip's hair was brown and curly and hers much darker. They both had blue eyes and the shape of their faces was similar. The physical resemblance was striking—a stranger would have known at once that they were related, might even have asked, Are you brother and sister? Are you twins? They were close in age— only around nine months apart; if you didn't know about the gap a stranger might well guess that they were twins.

'When you recovered consciousness, did you realise you had been in a coma?' she asked and he smiled, shaking his head.

'It was like waking up in the morning. I knew I had been asleep for a long time, I even had a vague memory of hearing voices—my mother's, Dad's, yours—but I was amazed when my nurse told me

I'd been out of it for so many days. Funnily enough,
I did remember her voice, too—I didn't feel she
was a stranger, although I'd never seen her before.
Her voice was very familiar, and I felt I'd known
her before somewhere.'

'She's nice, I liked her,' Nerissa said, still very
aware of Ben's dark, brooding presence. 'I talked
to you about her one day, told you she shaved you
and did a great job.'

He laughed, ran an exploratory hand along his
jaw. 'Mmm...feels OK.'

He was smiling and talking easily enough, but
under that lay something very different. He was
looking at her from a great distance now. The first
joy of seeing each other had drained away and they
were aware of being on ice floes drifting apart—
the gap between them had widened even more since
the last time they'd met.

Listening to Ben speculating on the reasons
behind Philip's 'accident', she had been afraid that
she would see despair and misery in Philip's eyes,
but there was something very different. Sadness,
yes, but resignation too, acceptance.

The door opened and Grace Thornton came in;
Philip looked at her, said, 'Hello, Mum. Had
lunch?'

'Sandwiches,' Nerissa told him, gently pulling her
hand free and getting up. 'Have my chair, Aunt
Grace.'

'Ben could get us another one,' Grace Thornton
said, sitting down just as Staff Nurse Courtney
came into the room.

'Three visitors aren't allowed, you know,' she said
lightly. 'One of you will have to go out for while,

and all of you will have to go soon. He's been ordered to rest so that he'll be able to face a whole string of tests tomorrow.'

'We won't stay,' Ben told her coolly. 'We don't want to tire him. Tomorrow afternoon OK to come again?'

She nodded. 'Fine. Around three would be perfect.' She walked to the bed and picked up Philip's wrist between finger and thumb. 'Now that he's out of danger the hospital rules apply again, though. Only two visitors to a patient at one time, remember, and please don't bring him food or drink, or stay more than an hour.'

'She's bossy,' Philip said, watching her glance at the watch pinned to her apron bib, begin counting his pulse-beats.

'Don't talk!' Staff Nurse said, a frown of concentration between her brows.

She put his hand back on the covers and walked to the end of the bed, wrote up his chart.

'Pulse-rate up,' she said. 'That's the excitement of having too many visitors! You see why we have to be careful and keep the rules?'

'Fuss, fuss, fuss,' Philip said.

'We must go,' Nerissa said. She wanted to kiss him but she couldn't, so she just looked at him from that great, silent distance, and Philip looked back at her.

'Goodbye,' he said, his blue eyes dark and melancholy.

He had said it before, but neither of them had ever meant it. They had not wanted to believe there was no hope, no future for them—they hadn't been able to live with the realisation. Suddenly she saw that that had changed, for both of them. Time, or reality, had done its work. They had given up struggling against the dictates of fate; they accepted what couldn't be altered.

Ben's long, powerful fingers closed over her arm, gripping her with angry ferocity.

'See you back at the farm,' he said to Grace Thornton and began to walk to the door, taking Nerissa with him. She didn't need to see his face to know he was angry with her; his body vibrated with it.

He put her into the front passenger seat of his car as if she were a child who had misbehaved, walked round and got in beside her, started the engine and drove off, his face harsh, set in cold lines.

'Nothing has changed, you know!' he muttered as he drove back towards the farm.

'Everything has changed,' she said huskily.

The car leapt forward as Ben put his foot down on the accelerator. 'Just because he has been very ill it doesn't mean the underlying situation has altered. You'd have to be crazy to think you could get away with it. I wouldn't let you, for one. Your aunt wouldn't let you, either—you must know that. She's a woman of principle; she wouldn't stand for it.'

'I know that,' Nerissa said.

'In fact, she's some sort of saint.'

'I know that, too.'

Ben looked down at her, his mouth crooked, cynical. 'You're a lot like her, you know.'

'My mother was her sister; it isn't so surprising!'

Ben's eyes hardened, silvery, fierce, scornful. 'That's what makes the whole thing so incredible! Her own sister! How can he live with himself? After doing what he did, how can he bear to face his wife...? How can she forgive him...? Hell! How can he even bear to look into the mirror every morning?'

White-faced, she looked out of the window at the passing countryside—the drystone walls rising between green meadows, the stubbled fields where wheat had once grown, a magpie on the wing, in a flash of black and white, between an oak and a half-dead elm blighted by Dutch elm disease, as so many were in England now.

'Haven't you ever done anything you regretted afterwards, Ben?' she whispered, her hands shaking in her lap. 'Haven't you ever given in to an impulse in a weak moment, then wished to God you hadn't? You've spent so much time in courts, I suppose, watching other people paying the price for their weaknesses, that you've forgotten that you're human, too. Well, I've got news for you—you aren't perfect either. None of us is. We all have a flaw somewhere, hidden or otherwise.'

He turned into the drive which led to the farm, his wheels grinding over the gravel, dust flying up around them.

'I've never been under any illusions about myself. I know I'm not perfect. Oh, I know what you're trying to do, Nerissa. You're looking for any weapon to attack me with because you don't want to face up to the truth about your father.'

Her breath caught. 'Don't...'

'Don't what?' Ben bit out. 'Call him that? He is your father, Nerissa, whether you like to admit it or not. Stop calling him Uncle John. He's your biological father, which makes Philip your biological half-brother, and no amount of protests or pretences on your part can ever change that.'

CHAPTER SIX

As soon as Ben had parked in front of the farm-house Nerissa opened her door and sprang out, but Ben was as fast on his feet and caught her before she made it to the front door.

'Stop running away from it! You've been doing that for far too long!'

His raised voice made her angry and nervous of being overheard by John Thornton, who might be somewhere around the farmhouse within earshot. She didn't want him to know what Ben thought of him. No doubt he guessed from the way Ben looked at him now and then, but she knew he would be hurt if he realised the depth of Ben's contempt for him.

'I don't want to talk about it!' She tried to pull her arm out of his grip but he simply tightened his hold, his long fingers like an iron bracelet.

'Can't you see that that's the problem? They had to tell you the truth once they realised you and Philip wanted to get married—and then as soon as they'd told you they buried it again, and the two of you accepted that—in effect you joined in the conspiracy of silence. But that's crazy. Hiding the truth didn't do anyone any good, did it? The only sane thing to do is to bring it all out into the open, talk about it, face what it means.'

'We have faced what it means! Why else did I go away? I had to be the one who went. Philip was

needed on the farm—I wasn't. But we couldn't bear
to go on seeing each other, not once we knew the
truth.' Her voice broke and she covered her face
with her hands. 'It was...unbearable...'

Ben put his arms round her and held her, one
hand behind her head, pushing it into his shoulder,
the other gently moving up and down her back,
stroking her like someone gentling a frightened
horse.

'Shh...don't cry...'

She choked back the tears that were threatening
and pushed him away, her face defiant.

'Why can't you leave me alone? If you didn't
keep hassling me I wouldn't get upset.' She walked
away, tried the front door and found it locked, got
out her key and let herself into the farmhouse, with
Ben following close on her heels.

They both paused, listening to the silence in the
house, the only sound the solemn ticking of a
grandfather clock in the hall. Nerissa walked
through to the kitchen; it was spotless and empty.
She filled the kettle and put it on the hob.

'I'm going to make some tea—do you want
some?' she asked over her shoulder without looking
at Ben.

'Please.' He walked to the window, opened it,
allowing the autumn wind to blow into the room,
bringing with it the earthy smell of fallen leaves
decaying, of the amber and dark red chrysanthemums which grew in Grace Thornton's little
garden and the sound of sheep on the hill,
leaves rustling, and somewhere, some way off, a
dog barking.

'Jess,' Nerissa said, listening, almost sick with relief because John Thornton was so far from the house and couldn't hear anything Ben might say about him.

Ben stared at the skyline, the dark, brooding presence of the hills above the house.

'I can see someone up there, right at the top, where we were this morning—I suppose that's him? I can't see well enough to be sure. It's someone in a tweed jacket; there's a dog, a black and white dog, running ahead of him, and a lot of sheep, straggling along in a great line.'

'He said he was going to move the flock into Great Meadow once he'd finished mending the walls.'

She set out cups, made the tea, found milk and filled a small jug, put out a sugar bowl.

Ben turned away to watch her and she found his brooding presence as disturbing as the ever-watchful hills that loomed over this house day and night.

His voice was quiet, dry. 'It isn't quite real, you know, Nerissa, this forgiving attitude of yours. I find it hard to believe that you don't burn with resentment for what he did to your mother, to you, to your aunt.'

'I've told you, I was angry, at first.' She had been torn apart, appalled, incredulous, stricken. 'I think I hated him for a while. I never wanted to see him again—I thought he was beneath contempt.' She looked at Ben wryly, grimacing. 'I suppose I thought exactly the way you do, for a while. But then Aunt Grace talked to me.'

She poured the tea and sat down at the kitchen table, her hands curled around her cup, staring at the floor.

'She tried to make me see how it had all happened. You know that her parents died not long after she got married? My mother—her sister, Ellen—was only seventeen then, in her last year at school, and so she came to live here. There were no other relatives, she had nowhere else to go, but there was plenty of room at Lantern, and she was company for Aunt Grace. You see how isolated the farm is; Aunt Grace sometimes missed having other people around, she admitted, in the beginning. She got used to being alone most of the time eventually, but in the early years of her marriage Uncle John was out working around the farm most of the time and she never had anyone to talk to. She was glad to have her sister around, especially as Aunt Grace was pregnant and it was a comfort to have another woman with her.'

'This baby was Philip, presumably?' Ben asked as she took a sip of tea.

She nodded, glad of the warmth of the tea. Although the kitchen was warm, she still felt chilled and she kept shivering.

'Philip was born that summer. It was a difficult birth—Aunt Grace was rushed off to hospital and had him there. She almost died during labour—that was why she never had another child; it was far too risky. She looks so strong and healthy, doesn't she? You would think she would have babies as easily as shelling peas! But she was warned not to have any more babies—it could happen again and next time she might not pull through. She was very upset

when they told her, and so was Uncle John. He was
alone here with Ellen. Aunt Grace said he was sick
with worry over her, over their baby, and——'

She broke off, shrugging, and Ben looked at her
with cold, arched brows, his expression derisive.

'Was that his excuse for seducing an adolescent
who was also his sister-in-law? Because he was so
worried about his wife?'

Nerissa heard the sarcasm, the scorn in the tone,
and looked angrily at him.

'He didn't give me any excuses when they told
us and I don't think he gave Aunt Grace any when
she found out. He just said he was desperately
sorry—he couldn't explain why it happened. He had
no excuse; he just begged her to forgive him and
said it would never happen again. And it wasn't an
affair; it only happened once.'

'Only once?' Ben repeated. 'Is that what he said?
And she believed him?'

'I don't know if she did at first—she was too
upset and angry, with both of them. But then she
talked to her doctor... He knew all about it, of
course—he was Ellen's doctor too. He was a junior
partner—the old doctor didn't go out on the
country rounds any more, he just dealt with
patients who could get to the surgery, and left the
outlying district visits to his young partner, who
was only in his late twenties then. He moved on
years ago, went to America, and works in New York
now. He was clever and ambitious, and quite ad-
vanced for the time—he knew something about
psychology, and he was broad-minded. He talked
her through her first reactions, told her that these
things happened more often than people realise...'

'I can vouch for that,' Ben said icily. 'My wife and my best friend—your uncle and his wife's sister. Yes, these things happen all the time. That doesn't make them any more forgivable.'

Nerissa looked at him through her lashes, seeing the taut structure of his face, the hard eyes, the tense mouth. How much of his bitter contempt for her uncle was because her twisted family history reminded him of his first marriage and the betrayal that had ended it?

Ben talked so dismissively of pride—the pride that had made her family fight to keep their secret, the pride that had done such damage to her and Philip when they'd grown up and fallen in love, not knowing they were brother and sister. Yet Ben was driven by pride too—the betrayal by his wife and his best friend had given his pride a terrible wound from which he still hadn't recovered.

'Sometimes,' she said quietly, 'forgiveness is the only way to heal yourself.'

He stared at her, his expression not changing, and she sighed. He wasn't going to listen, or, if he did, take seriously what she said. His pride was monolithic, unbending.

'Aunt Grace's doctor told her that husbands find the whole process of having a baby almost as much of a strain as their wives do,' she went on after a minute. 'Men aren't actually involved in what happens—or weren't, then. They weren't allowed to be present during labour—it was all a female mystery and the father had no place in it.'

'I must admit I'd find that intolerable,' said Ben soberly. 'I'd want to be there when my child was born; it's such a big moment, I'd have to share it, and after all it takes two to make a baby. If you're in on the conception you should be in on the birth.'

Nerissa felt a queer little leap of her heart and was taken aback. Why should that make her feel so odd? She had married him, slept with him, but it had never occurred to her that she might one day have Ben's child. Did he want children, then?

What would a child of Ben's look like? Dark, tall, wiry, with those grey eyes——

She broke off the thought, very flushed, and hurriedly went back to what she had been saying.

'Once the baby actually arrives, apparently, men sometimes feel left out, ignored—suddenly their wives don't have any time for them, they're too absorbed in this new arrival, and then after all the adrenalin of waiting for the birth there's a terrible sense of let-down. They get depressed but nobody is taking any notice of them, nobody realises they feel very low. And that is when they sometimes look elsewhere for comfort.'

Ben's cool, sardonic eyes stayed on her face. He was sitting opposite her at the table, not drinking his own tea, his lean body lounging back in the chair, his hands linked behind his head and his long legs crossed, his foot rhythmically swinging back and forth impatiently, in a gesture very like the angry swish of a cat's tail.

'Sounds to me like special pleading—men closing ranks, protecting each other's backs. If my wife had a baby I wouldn't go looking for another woman.'

'You're stronger than Uncle John . . .'

Ben snapped, 'Don't keep calling him that! It continues the lie!'

Her flush deepened, her eyes angry too. 'I can't call him anything else! I've called him that all my life, for one thing; that's how I think of him. I couldn't start calling him something else—and, for another thing, if I did it would start tongues wagging. Nobody around here knows—the doctor never told anyone, and my mother went away... In fact, she left without telling anyone she was going. She went to London, got a job working in a hotel, and that was where she met the man she married, the man I always believed was my father.'

'Did he know she was already pregnant?'

She nodded. 'Aunt Grace said her sister told him the truth and he said he didn't mind, he would take care of both of us. He loved my mother very much; Aunt Grace says he would have done anything for her. When she died, he was distraught—her death changed everything for him. For one thing, he couldn't take care of me on his own.' She paused, biting her lip. 'And I don't think he wanted me with him any more. I was a living reminder of what he'd lost. If I'd been his child, that might have been a comfort, but as it was...well, he felt he had no responsibility for me, so he brought me back here and Aunt Grace agreed to bring me up. He would never have come back for me, even if he hadn't died, I suppose.'

'Whatever he said to your mother, he must have been jealous of John Thornton,' Ben speculated aloud.

Nerissa pushed away her empty cup, her eyes lowered, a dark fan of lashes brushing each cheek.

'She must have been in love with him,' she murmured huskily.

'With her husband?' Ben sounded dubious.

'With Uncle John.'

Ben started intently, his grey eyes penetrating, shrewd. 'Is that what your aunt told you?'

Nerissa shook her head. 'She never tried to explain her sister's motives. I didn't ask, either. I just worked it out for myself, from what I know about Uncle John and Aunt Grace.'

'Isn't it obvious that you don't know them at all?' Ben broke out sharply and she drew back, flinching from his angry voice.

She swallowed, eyes flickering in nervous reaction, then muttered, 'I know one thing—he would never have forced himself on an unwilling girl so she must have wanted what happened!'

Ben grimaced, subsiding in his chair, his momentary burst of anger over. 'OK, you may be right about that. But she was young and impressionable—he could have seduced her; she might not have realised what was happening...'

'I have a strong feeling it was the other way around,' Nerissa said bleakly. 'And I think Aunt Grace believes that too. I think my mother was in love with him and seduced him—maybe without intending to, just following her instincts—I don't know, but I don't believe Uncle John would have made the first move. It simply isn't in character. He's far too diffident; Aunt Grace has always been the dominant one in that partnership.'

'Was your mother like her, then?'

Nerissa shook her head. 'No, very different—she was tiny, rather frail. She died of leukaemia, you know. She had probably had it for years before they discovered what was wrong with her. I sometimes

wonder if that wasn't why she was so reckless—
why all this happened. Maybe she had some inkling
that she might die young, and she was desperate to
live while she still could.'

'How old was she when she died?'

'Only twenty-one.' Nerissa heard herself say it,
and suddenly realised how young that was—she was
older than that now herself. Twenty-one was no age
at all, was it?

Ben's face grew sombre. 'Poor girl.' He stared at
her, frowning, his eyes searching her face. 'And
you're like her? It's true, you are delicate—you get
colds easily and you're very slight in build—but
you're like your aunt too, in other ways. You have
her tough core, her ability to cope with things.'

Her eyes softened. 'I'm flattered; I love Aunt
Grace. If she hadn't been able to forgive what happened, if she hadn't taken me in...I might have
ended up in an orphanage and had a very unhappy
childhood.'

'Yes,' said Ben slowly. 'She's a wonderful
woman. I admire her; I wish I had her strength of
character. I don't find it so easy to forgive injuries.'

She didn't need to be told that. She knew how
iron-hard Ben's pride was, and how deep the roots
of his bitterness ran.

'I don't believe she found it easy—I think she
worked at it,' Nerissa told him. 'She never blamed
anybody when she talked to me about it. She just
told me what had happened and tried to explain
why. That's why I'm sure my mother made all the
moves. I sensed Aunt Grace believed that. She told
me Uncle John was lonely and upset, worried—he
lost his head. Almost at once, though, he realised

what he had done and was stricken with guilt, because it was always Aunt Grace he loved.'

'I don't buy that,' Ben said coldly. 'If he loved his wife, how could he sleep with her sister? Oh, I've no doubt that's what he told his wife, but he doesn't convince me. I think the truth is he was here, on his own, with a pretty girl who made it obvious that she liked him a lot, and the temptation was irresistible—but if he had really loved his wife so much he would never have been tempted.'

Nerissa had thought that too once. At first. But Aunt Grace had forgiven her husband and gone on loving him—how could Nerissa refuse to do the same?

'He's weak,' she said sadly. 'He fell from grace...'

'Like Lucifer, the dark angel,' Ben said wryly.

She half smiled; the description was so far from the reality of the man Ben was talking about. 'I don't know about that. Unlike Lucifer Uncle John is human, and as soon as he had started his affair with my mother he stopped it because it really was Aunt Grace he loved. The real tragedy was that my mother was already pregnant.'

'That must have been a blinding shock for him, when she told him!'

Nerissa nodded. 'Especially as she didn't say a word for almost three months.'

'Three months?' echoed Ben.

'Don't forget, my mother was only seventeen— she apparently didn't realise she was pregnant for quite a time, and was afraid to go to the doctor to ask even when she began to suspect. She didn't tell

Uncle John until she was nearly three months pregnant. When he got over the shock, he realised he had to tell Aunt Grace the truth. He hadn't confessed the affair before; that was when he told Aunt Grace about it. It was Aunt Grace who took her to see the doctor. The pregnancy was confirmed and a few days later my mother ran away. She left a note and vanished, and they didn't know where to find her. She wrote months later, when she was getting married, and she let them know when I was born, but she never came back here again and the first time they set eyes on me was when my father brought me here after she died.'

'Had he let them know she was dead?'

'No. Apparently, he buried her without anyone else being there, just him by the graveside, and the next morning he brought me here without warning them that we were coming. I expect he was afraid that if he let them know in advance they would tell him not to come, or think up some reason why they couldn't take me.'

Ben stared at her, frowning, as if trying to imagine what she had looked like then, a small, delicate child with no idea of the storms raging around her. Nerissa had often looked back to that day herself, the first day she ever saw Lantern Farm or the family there. It seemed a century ago, and yet at the same time it was like yesterday.

Ben slowly said, 'It must have knocked them for six to hear that Ellen was dead.'

Nerissa nodded. 'Aunt Grace loved my mother—she had never stopped loving her, in spite of what happened. I don't think she blamed her, any more than she blamed Uncle John—she tried to under-

stand, and she forgave. That's what makes Aunt
Grace such a special person—she never harbours
grudges or wants revenge for anything.'

'A woman without pride,' Ben said and his tone
was odd; she couldn't tell if that was awe or contempt in his voice. Then he added softly, 'A rose
without thorns.'

'She has pride,' Nerissa said flatly. 'It isn't your
sort of pride, that's all. Aunt Grace has too much
pride, in fact—too much to refuse to forgive
someone when they say they're sorry, or go on
nursing a grievance for years. She always says life
is too short; she says bearing a grudge is like having
a thorn under your skin—she can't understand why
people do that. It's as much them who suffer.
They're in pain all the time they refuse to forgive
and forget. That's why she didn't even hesitate—
she told my father she would keep me, bring me
up as her own child, although she hadn't had time
to think about it. She didn't need to think. She told
me that it wasn't just that I was her husband's child,
I was her sister's, too; I was family; I belonged with
them. So my mother's husband left me with her
and went away.'

'Do you remember him?'

'Very dimly. I was too young to remember
much—it's almost as if I started living when I came
here.' She looked down at her cup. 'Do you want
some more tea?'

'No, thanks.'

She got up and automatically washed out the cups
and saucers, emptied the teapot, tidied the kitchen
again. 'I'll do some housework for Aunt Grace,'
she thought aloud. 'It worries her that she isn't

getting the vacuuming and dusting done.' She looked at Ben. 'What will you do this afternoon? Why not go for a ride? Uncle John won't mind if you borrow his horse again—he lent Oliver to you before, remember? The black hunter? You can saddle him yourself, can't you?'

Ben nodded, his mouth crooked with amusement and mockery. 'Didn't I say you were like your aunt? One minute you're talking about a family tragedy, the next you're calmly deciding to do the housework and bossing me about.'

She shrugged, half smiling too. 'If you don't want to ride, don't. I don't care what you do.'

She felt the atmosphere change, the temperature between them come down with a thud. Looking with apprehension at Ben, she saw that his little smile had gone. His face had hardened, gone cold, his eyes like daggers.

'I'm well aware of that,' he bit out through his teeth.

Bewildered, she stared back at him—what on earth was he talking about now? He was like a weather-vane lately; he swung from mood to mood without rhyme or reason, and certainly without warning. What had she said to make him so angry?

'You don't give a damn about me in any way, do you, Nerissa?' he snarled and her nerves jangled like alarm bells.

He took a step toward her and she involuntarily took a step backwards, her blue eyes wide and dark.

'Don't shrink away from me!' he muttered, and she froze on the spot, trying not to tremble in case he noticed it. He stood in front of her, staring, and

Nerissa looked down, her lashes veiling her eyes, feeling her heart beating too rapidly against her ribs.

'Stop biting my head off, Ben!' she said huskily. 'What's the matter with you? It was just a casual remark—I wasn't getting at you, or being nasty. You said you didn't want me bossing you around, so I said——'

'I know what you said, and I know what you meant. The truth comes out in these casual remarks. You don't care what I do, you said—and that's the truth. If I vanished tomorrow you wouldn't turn a hair, any more than you care a damn about the man you believed was your father. Out of sight, out of mind. You're still obsessed with your half-brother—you've never stopped thinking about him. The minute you had an excuse you came running back here, not even bothering to let me know you were going, or why. I'm beginning to think you don't even want to get over him, even though you keep saying you know there's no future for the two of you. I saw you together today and I felt sick because it was so clear how you both still felt.'

Nerissa looked up at him then, her eyes dark with shock and terrible, blinding pain. It was in that instant that she realised he was a million miles from the truth. It came as a thunderclap to her. Why hadn't she realised long ago?

She was no longer in love with Philip.

Oh, she loved him—she always would. He was her brother, her friend, the closest person on earth to her; he had shared her childhood and her growing years—they had spent most of their lives together, roaming these hills, riding on their ponies through the heather, swimming in the clear, cool stream which came down from the very highest peaks above the house. Philip was her other self, her mirror image, her twin.

But she was not in love with him.

It was that closeness that had deceived her for so long, in fact. She had mistaken her deep affection for something else, and that had made her misunderstand the intense desire she had felt for Ben from the moment they first met.

She had told herself it was mere chemistry, a physical instinct, a sexual drive which had nothing to do with the emotions. She wanted Ben because he was an attractive male, not because of the man himself, not because she was in love with him.

She had had tunnel vision—so blinkered by her belief that Philip was the only man in the world for her that she couldn't see anything else. Why had it taken so long for the blinkers to come off?

They were off now. She was able to see the truth and she was stunned by it—like a survivor of a bomb attack she was blind, deaf, dumb with shock, groping in a world turned crazy, trying to come to terms with her new realisation.

She was in love with Ben. She had been for a long time.

'Oh, to hell with you!' Ben broke out suddenly. 'I'm going back to London. Come with me or stay, just as you like—but if you stay, Nerissa, our marriage is over!'

He turned on his heel and walked out, ran upstairs. Nerissa stood in the kitchen, her blue eyes dark with shock.

When she heard him come downstairs again, she went out into the hall in a hurry. He was carrying his suitcase and she felt a pang of dismay as she realised he had meant it; he was really going.

'Ben, listen...I can't come now. How can I when they need me? But...' she began, and he turned a grim face to her.

'No buts, Nerissa. I meant what I said. I'm sick of this charade of a marriage. I can't live with it any more.'

He was gone a moment later, the front door slamming behind him, and she stood rooted to the spot, white-faced and stunned. She heard the car start, the engine roar as he put his foot down on the accelerator, the sound of the wheels churning gravel as he set off along the drive.

Ben had left her.

CHAPTER SEVEN

AUNT GRACE came home some hours later to find that Nerissa had cleaned the whole house from top to bottom and was in the kitchen, preparing dinner.

Nerissa heard her moving about and put on the kettle for tea. Aunt Grace appeared in the doorway a few moments later, saying, 'Well, you've been busy! You are a good girl. I was just thinking to myself, Well, I'll have to get down to it tomorrow! And here you've been, polishing the whole place like a new pin!'

Nerissa managed a smile for her, then bent to taste the soup she was making in a big, copper-bottomed pan. 'There's tea in the pot; I just made it.'

'I was dying for a cup!' Grace Thornton sat down with a sigh of relief and poured herself a cup of tea. 'What's that you're cooking? It smells grand.'

'Uncle John left a trug of very ripe tomatoes on the table, so I reckoned he meant us to use them tonight and soup seemed a good idea. I've put in some basil from your herb garden.'

Aunt Grace nodded approval. 'We've a glut of tomatoes this autumn—it's a good way of using them up. If I had the time I should bottle some, and make a few jars of pickle—I've got plenty of shallots and nasturtium seeds, too. I usually try to make some tomato and onion pickle around this time of year, remember?'

'Yes,' Nerissa said absently, thinking of Ben, then caught on to what her aunt had been saying and said, 'I could do that for you tomorrow while you're visiting Philip!'

'Ben might want to take you out for a drive. He will get very bored up here, doing nothing.' Aunt Grace drank some more tea, said casually, 'I noticed his car wasn't outside. Has he gone for a drive on his own?'

'He's gone back to London,' Nerissa said, her back to her aunt as she opened the oven to check on the crown of lamb roasting in it. Heat rushed out, making her pale face flush.

'Is he coming back?' Her aunt's voice was sharp; she had picked up something in Nerissa's tone.

'No.' Nerissa basted the meat, turned the potatoes and sliced parsnips cooking in another dish to make sure they were evenly browned, shut the door and straightened up.

'What's the matter, Nerissa?' Grace Thornton was watching her intently. Nerissa kept her face averted, tried to make her voice calm as she answered.

'He's very busy; he had to get back.' While she'd been working around the house she had thought about what she would say. She didn't want her uncle and aunt to know that her marriage was in any danger or to guess that Ben had given her that ultimatum—demanded that she choose, in effect, between him and her family. They had enough guilt to carry already. They didn't need any more.

'I thought he was going to stay for the rest of the week?' She wasn't fooling her aunt; Grace

Thornton was far too sensitive to moods—those penetrating eyes of hers didn't miss a thing.

'He meant to but——' Nerissa stopped, her voice breaking. Talking about Ben meant thinking about Ben—and that hurt. Agony throbbed inside her mind like a great, dark bruise every time she remembered Ben had left her.

'Nerissa, love . . . what's wrong?'

Her aunt's sympathy was too much to bear. It undermined her, made it impossible to hide her misery. She covered her face with her hands, unable to control the shuddering of her body.

Aunt Grace gave a distressed cry, hurried over, put her arms round her. 'Don't cry, love. It can't be that bad.'

Nerissa leaned on her for a minute, then pulled away, choking back her sobs.

'He's left me, Aunt Grace!'

Grace Thornton took hold of her niece's chin and firmly dried her face as if she were five years old, then, still holding her, looked into her wet blue eyes in searching insistence.

'Why, love? What's gone wrong between you?'

Nerissa shook her head helplessly. She couldn't explain; it was too personal, too complicated.

'Is this over Philip?'

Her aunt's shrewd question made her breath catch. She didn't reply, but then she didn't have to—Grace was closely watching every expression that crossed her face.

'It is,' Grace concluded, frowning. She gave a long sigh. 'We shouldn't have asked you to come!'

Nerissa stirred, her eyes angry. 'Of course you should! He's my brother; you had to let me know how ill he was—and I had to come! If he had died I'd never have forgiven myself if I hadn't been here!'

It was the first time she had ever called Philip her brother and her aunt's face registered the fact, a ripple of shock passing over her features.

Grace slowly nodded. 'Yes, you had the right to know. But Ben resented... He didn't want you to come?'

She nodded. 'He thinks I... still——' She broke off, biting her lip—she couldn't put it into words, certainly not to Philip's mother, their father's wife. The whole complex muddle was too brittle; she was afraid of what she might precipitate if she said too much.

Grace Thornton felt for her hand, patted it gently. 'Of course, he knows about Philip... and he suspects you still feel the same way?'

Nerissa half laughed, close to hysteria. Aunt Grace knew. Why had she tried to save her feelings? She should have realised it wasn't necessary to put it into words—Aunt Grace always heard what you didn't say; she read your thoughts in your eyes, in the tone of your voice. She saw so few people up here, along this remote border between Scotland and England, with the wind and rain blowing off the moors more often than not, and yet with such scarce material to practise on Grace Thornton had somehow managed to become expert at people-watching. She liked people, that was her secret, thought Nerissa. She liked them and cared about them; she wasn't blinded by self the way most people were.

The way I have been, Nerissa realised with a sinking feeling. I've been so obsessed by what I wanted, what I felt, that I haven't been able to see anything else.

I haven't seen Ben, thought about Ben's feelings; I've no idea what goes on inside Ben. I've lived with him for months—he has been my lover, my husband and yet I know very little about the man behind the façade the rest of the world sees.

'Go after him,' Aunt Grace said and Nerissa looked at her, startled, wildly shaking her head.

'I can't!'

'Why not, for heaven's sake?' Grace sounded impatient, which was very unusual for her. She was one of the most patient women Nerissa had ever met.

'How can I? I can't leave while Philip is still so ill.'

'Never mind Philip,' Grace said briskly. 'He's going to be fine now he's out of the coma. I saw his specialist this evening, just before I left. He says he believes we'll see a very rapid climb back to health. Philip is young and strong and very fit. You don't need to worry about him. And anyway, he isn't your priority, Nerissa. Your husband is. Go after him.' Grace Thornton paused, stared at her fixedly. 'Unless you don't want him. Do you want him, Nerissa?'

Pride held her silent. She bit down on her lip, a little coin of scarlet in each cheek.

Her aunt waited a moment then said, 'I've seen the two of you together—I think you do. If you love him, don't let him go, Nerissa. Fight for him.'

Nerissa took a deep breath, flicked her a quick look. 'Is that what you did?'

Grace gave a wry little smile, nodded. 'And don't think it was easy for me, because it wasn't. When John told me what had gone on between him and Ellen, I wanted to kill the pair of them.'

'I can understand that.' Nerissa knew now how she would feel if she found out that Ben had had an affair with someone else since they'd got married.

Grace Thornton made a face. 'Oh, aye, I were as jealous as sin, and very angry. But, thank God, I had a lot of common sense and I didn't follow my first impulse—which was to tell them both to get out and ask John for a divorce.'

That surprised Nerissa and her aunt saw her startled face and laughed with gritty humour.

'Did you think I was too saintly? Nay, lass, to tell you t'truth I wanted to beat seven bells out of both of them! It were on the tip of my tongue to say, Get out of my house and never let me see either of you again. I don't know how I held it back. But I had practical things to do—I had to take Ellen to the doctor and make sure she really was carrying a child, and I had my own baby to take care of. I was kept too busy to have time to brood and work myself up into a tearing rage. And before I'd decided what to do Ellen bolted, and I realised that whatever he had done I still loved John and I didn't want to lose him. Ellen made it easy for me, poor girl; she made my mind up for me, in a way. I think she loved him too, or she'd never have done what she did.'

Nerissa looked at her in disbelief. 'You always seem so calm about it! How can you be so detached?'

'After over twenty years? You know what they say—time's a great healer. I wasn't detached in the beginning, believe me, but when you love someone you can swallow your pride and put your anger aside. You have to if you're going to be able to go on living with them. You can't live with someone you're that angry with—it's corrosive; it destroys any chance of happiness the two of you might have.'

'Easier said then done, though.'

'Oh, aye. I didn't say it were easy, love. Just that you've a choice to make—if you love him, you've got to work it out between you. At first it's a struggle every day to hold your tongue and keep your temper, but as the days go by it gets easier and easier. Loving is the key, Nerissa. You have to want to make it work.'

'I do,' Nerissa admitted huskily.

'Then you'll have to be the one who does the running after—it's too late tonight, but John shall drive you to the station tomorrow morning and you can get the train to London.'

Nerissa still hesitated. 'I've hardly had a chance to talk to Philip yet, though. I ought to see him one more time—say goodbye to him.'

'I'll say it for you.' Grace's level eyes were challenging, steady. 'It's best, love. For both of you. You know it is. I think you're both over it; you've come to terms with the way it has to be, but it's too soon to be safe—you need to keep a distance between you yet. One day you'll be able to meet as

brother and sister and never remember the way
things were once.'

Nerissa nodded bleakly.

'I'm sorry, love,' her aunt said in a low voice,
patting her hand. 'It was all our fault. We had no
business keeping it a secret, not from you two, at
any rate. We should have told you when you were
children, but it never entered our heads that it would
ever be a problem. I blame myself. It was to protect
my pride that we never let on that you were John's.
He would have loved to tell the world you were
his...'

'Would he?' Nerissa smiled, a quivering
movement of the mouth which wasn't reflected in
her uncertain eyes. Grace nodded her head
insistently.

'He loves you—you know that! He kept it secret
for my sake—don't ever blame your father, blame
me! He knew it would hurt my pride for all the
neighbours and family to know about him and
Ellen. I'd have felt humiliated—I'd have thought
they were all whispering and laughing at me behind
my back. I made it a condition, you see, for forgiving him. That was wrong of me, to make con-
ditions—but I did. I told him, We'll forget it ever
happened, but nobody else must ever know. He
agreed. Well, it never occurred to either of us that
Ellen would die so soon and you would come to
live with us.'

Nerissa searched her face. 'It must have been a
very hard thing to do, to take me in!'

'I can't say it was,' Grace said calmly, smiling at
her affectionately. 'You were such a pretty little
thing, just a baby, and you looked lost that day you

arrived. You were looking around for your
mother—you didn't even know she was dead, poor
lamb. I'd have had to have had a heart of stone to
turn you away. I should have had the courage to
tell you John was your father, though. I wish to
God I had. I never meant to hurt you, though,
Nerissa. I love you; you know that.'

'Of course I know!' Nerissa impulsively hugged
her. 'Don't ever blame yourself—I do understand.
I'm sure I'd have felt exactly the same in your place.
I don't think I could have been as generous. You're
the only mother I can remember and you gave me
a wonderful childhood, both me and Philip. You're
a very special person, Aunt Grace, and I love you.'

She hardly slept at all that night; she was possessed
by images of Ben, tortured by memories of their
time together. All the time she had wasted! If she
could only have that time back!

She wished she had gone with him. She should
have packed after talking to Aunt Grace and left
at once, not stayed on for a last night here. If Ben
had meant what he said their marriage was over;
he would divorce her.

But had he meant it? She kept remembering the
harsh sound of his voice, the hardness of his face,
the sense of finality in the way he'd slammed the
front door as he'd left. Her heart sank and she felt
sick. Yes, he had meant it! she thought grimly. It
was too late already.

Yet she couldn't give up hope—not yet. She had
to try to get him back—she wasn't letting him go
that easily.

Early next day she hugged Aunt Grace and said goodbye, sent loving messages to Philip, and drove off with John Thornton to catch her train back to London.

It was an express train, stopping only at major city stations. Their names flashed past without Nerissa noticing them—Newcastle, York, and so on southwards, rushing past autumnal landscapes and city suburbs in a cool, watery sunlight.

She reached London just after lunchtime and took a taxi to her home, her nerves stretched to breaking-point the closer she came to seeing Ben. She hadn't let him know she was coming; what she had to say to him could only be said face to face.

The sun was shining as they turned into the street where she had been living with Ben for the past few months. It looked exactly as it had the day she'd left to rush up north—there were the pigeons, their soft grey feathers iridescent in sunlight, strutting and cooing on the gables of the houses. The smoky scent of chrysanthemums was in every garden and the gutters were filling up with fallen leaves, golden and brown and russet, which rustled and scuttled along like living things, crunched under the wheels of cars, filled up the gardens and porches of the street.

'Which one is it, missus?' the taxi driver asked over his shoulder, his engine idling as he cruised along, staring at the houses.

'The second on the left,' Nerissa said, staring at the windows tensely. Was Ben in? Was he watching her? What would he be thinking? How was he going to look at her? What would he say?

After she paid off the taxi she carried her case up the path, pulses flickering, waiting for the front door to open, for Ben to appear.

She had thought through this moment a hundred times, but she still had no idea how he was going to react to the sight of her.

She put down her case, listening for the sound of steps inside. There wasn't a sound. She hadn't expected him to be out. She had been too intent on seeing him again; she had simply believed he would be there, in the house, when she arrived.

Slowly, she got out her keys and unlocked the door. Still not a sound.

She walked in, put her case down again, stood listening to the silence of the house. After a minute she went into the kitchen—it was immaculate, nothing out of place, everything shining and spotless, nothing in the dishwasher, no sign of anyone having used a cup or a plate that morning.

She looked into the other ground-floor rooms. They were all as pristine. Nobody had sat on a chair or sofa, there was no imprint of a body, no newspapers flung down, as Ben often did before hurrying out, no books piled on a table, no sign of him at all.

This was not one of the days their cleaner worked, though. She couldn't have been in here this morning, tidying up after Ben.

Frowning, Nerissa went upstairs into their bedroom. The bed was as smooth as glass. If anyone had slept in it last night the bed had been made since, with clean linen, and she couldn't believe Ben had done it. It had that practised perfection she recognised as the work of her cleaner.

She felt the pillow lightly with the fingers of one hand. Cool, unwrinkled—nobody had slept on that last night. It was freshly, crisply ironed and untouched.

She looked into the wardrobe, checked through Ben's clothes. The ones he had brought to Lantern Farm were not hanging there—nor were any of his shirts or underclothes in the laundry basket in the *en-suite* bathroom. The bath was dry and so was the bathroom washbasin; the towels on the heated rail were all new and unused.

There was no sign of his suitcase in the small room next door which they used as a linen-room, airing cupboard and storeroom for luggage and anything else that wasn't actually in use.

She hurried through the other rooms upstairs and then stood on the landing, her face pale and blank.

Ben had not been here last night. Where could he have gone after he left the farm?

Horrific thoughts rushed through her mind. What if he had crashed his car? What if he had been killed? Lay dying in some hospital? Or, even if he was only injured, would he give her name? Ask anyone to let her know where he was?

He would think she was still at Lantern Farm. As far as Ben was aware their marriage was over; she had chosen to stay with Philip. He wouldn't want her if he had had an accident.

What am I going to do? she thought desperately.

She had to find out if he had got back to London or not. Of course! He would be keeping in touch with his chambers; he wouldn't just vanish and not let them know where he was.

She ran back downstairs and went into his study, but before she rang his chambers she turned off the answerphone and pressed the playback switch. He might have left a message for her.

The first message was from Helen Manners, her voice hurried, soft, intimate. 'Ben, ring me as soon as you can. I need to talk to you urgently—I'll be at the office until six and after that at home.'

When had that been recorded? Today?

Ben had come back here from The Hague, after all, had played the messages on the phone then, wiped the tape and reset the machine, and she knew that he could ring this number and have any messages played back to him, wherever he was in the world, then reset the machine by remote control. Had he been doing so? Or were these old messages from days ago?

Another message had begun—from a legal colleague wanting Ben to ring him back to make a date for a game of squash—then there were several others, all for Ben. Nerissa had few friends—those she did have were the wives of Ben's colleagues and friends and Ben was always included in invitations from them.

Helen Manners had rung again. 'Ben, this is Helen again—you said you'd be picking up your messages so I thought you'd be in touch, but you haven't. It's absolutely vital I talk to you. Please ring me at once.'

That was it. The tape stopped automatically; no more messages had been recorded. It wound itself back and Nerissa reset it.

She hesitated, biting her lip, then rang his firm, asked to speak to him without giving her own name, using a low, husky voice she hoped they wouldn't recognise.

The receptionist who answered the phone in Ben's chambers politely told her that Ben was not available. He wasn't in chambers that day; he would not be back later and no, she couldn't say when he would be back.

'He's taking the week off, visiting relatives up north,' she finally admitted.

Nerissa asked for his secretary; she might know something the receptionist didn't. Whether Helen Manners would tell Ben's wife anything was another matter. She was still very hostile to Nerissa.

'She isn't here either,' said the receptionist. 'She rang in this morning to say she was taking the rest of the week off too, as her boss wasn't going to be needing her.'

Nerissa put the phone down and stood by the window, staring out into the back garden of the house. Ben didn't have much time for gardening; he had had a large stone terrace built along the back of the house, with stone steps leading down to a long lawn which a gardener mowed once a week in spring and summer. There were no flowerbeds, but a few flowering shrubs had been planted along the edges of the lawn—blue and pink lace-cap hydrangeas, which were covered with flowers at the moment, dwarf azaleas which in the spring had a riot of colour, and flowering cherry with its cat-like scent and dusty pink bells in May.

This afternoon there was a melancholy look to the place—dead leaves blew across the grass, the willow drooped, bare and dejected, in one corner, moss was growing over the face of a statue by the small goldfish pond at the end of the lawn.

If Ben hadn't gone to work and wasn't at home—where was he?

Her heart turned over painfully, a faint flush creeping into her pale face. Perhaps he had relented? Had gone back to the farm to see her?

She hurriedly began dialling again. Grace Thornton answered the phone and Nerissa knew Ben had not been there from the surprised tone of her aunt's voice.

'Oh, hello, love—is everything OK?'

'I thought I'd ring and let you know I'd had a good journey and arrived safely,' Nerissa said huskily, her anxiety beginning again now she knew Ben wasn't there.

'Have you talked to Ben?'

'Not yet, he's at work,' lied Nerissa. 'How's Philip?'

'He's fine. I spent a couple of hours with him this morning, and I shall go back later this evening.'

'Well, give him and Uncle John my love. I'll be in touch. Bye.'

She hung up and stood by the window, staring out. Ben was not at work, he was not here, he was not at the farm—where was he?

If he had picked up his messages today he might have rung Helen Manners, of course. There had been urgency in her voice.

Nerissa flicked open Ben's address book which lay on top of his desk; she turned the pages until she found Helen's home number.

Helen lived in Highgate, close to the famous cemetery where Karl Marx and so many other

eminent Victorians were buried in imposing marble
tombs. Helen's flat overlooked one side of the
cemetery; she had moved in there only recently and
given a house-warming party to which Ben had
taken Nerissa. Helen had had the flat redecorated
in cool, pastel shades and her furniture and fittings
were ultra-modern, but she had managed to make
them look a natural interior for the high Victorian
house of which she had the top floor. She had good
taste, Nerissa couldn't deny that—any more than
she could deny Helen's cold, Nordic beauty.

Her dislike of the other woman made Nerissa
hesitate before dialling the number. She hated the
idea of Helen knowing that she had no idea where
her husband could be—she was under no illusions
as to the other woman's reaction. Helen would
jump to obvious conclusions, guess that they'd
quarrelled, start hoping that their marriage was
already on the rocks.

From the minute they'd met Nerissa had suspected that Helen was in love with Ben. It was the
only explanation for her icy hostility. Nerissa had
seen her talking to clients, to other lawyers, other
girls who worked for the firm—Helen could be
charming, smooth, blandly pleasant.

But never to her. The reason was obvious, and
Nerissa was reluctant to let Helen know that she
had no idea where Ben was—the other woman was
bound to put two and two together, guess that there
was trouble between them and, no doubt, exult in
it.

But if anyone knew where Ben was, it would
be Helen.

She picked the phone up hurriedly, dialled. Nobody answered. Helen wasn't in. Nerissa put the phone down again, face blank. What now? Could Ben have gone back to The Hague without letting his firm know? She couldn't believe he would do that.

Oh, where was he? Where could he have gone? His sister's house? He and Jenny weren't very close—Ben rarely visited her and her husband—but he might have gone there. Nerissa couldn't face ringing her sister-in-law, though; it would be a harder thing to do than ringing Helen. It would be too humiliating; her pride wouldn't let her pick up the phone.

Who else might know where he was? One of his friends? Some of them had been quite kind to her and one or two of their wives had been friendly enough, but none of them was close enough for her to want to admit she had actually lost her husband, had no idea where he was at the moment. They would be bound to ask questions, and after-wards... She winced at the thought of the talk it would cause, the whisper of gossip and specu-lation, the way people would look at her, at Ben.

If Ben came back...

She couldn't do that to him, wound his pride by exposing him to the curiosity of his friends and their wives.

She looked away from the wedding photo on his desk, walked out of his study without any idea of where she was going, what she ought to do.

She found herself in the sitting-room and stood at the window, staring out into the autumnal London street, realising how few friends she had in the city. There was no one for her to confide in, no one to advise her what to do. Since marrying Ben she had plenty of acquaintances—his friends and their wives, women who were pleasant if they met in the street shopping, who might invite her round for a coffee, chat to her across a dinner-table. But she hadn't made any close friends. She was far too shy for one thing, and for another...

She closed her eyes, angry with herself. The real, underlying reason why she had no close friends and could confide in no one was because her body had been here, in London, but her whole heart and mind had still been obsessed with Philip. She had been living with Ben, sleeping in his bed, making love to him—but in a sense she had still been elsewhere, on the moors and wind-swept heights of her childhood.

From now on that was going to change! She was going to make friends, get closer to people, build a new life here in London. If Ben came back...

Her eyes were fixed on the street without seeing anything. A car pulled up outside the house. She was thinking sluggishly, her brain registering the make and colour slowly. Then she realised... Ben's car! The driver's door opened and Ben got out of it.

Her heart began beating wildly, fiercely. Her eyes ate him up; he looked OK, no sign of injury, his suit as immaculately pressed as ever. He walked round the car, the wind blowing his black hair back from his smoothly shaved face, bent, opened the front passenger door.

Nerissa's heart stopped violently, for a beat of time, as she saw who Ben had brought home with him.

Helen Manners slid her long, smooth legs out and got up, not a blonde hair out of place, make-up perfect, wearing a clinging cranberry-red dress in wild jersey, the lines of her lovely body accentuated by the close-fitting material.

She looked fabulous. Nerissa hated her.

Ben shut the car door, walked round to the back and got his suitcase out of the boot of the car, locked the car, then he and Helen walked together up the path to the front door, talking, laughing, their attention totally riveted on each other, in an intimacy that excluded the rest of the world.

He's been with her all night, Nerissa thought. Why else has he still got his suitcase with him? He certainly hasn't been here. He's arrived back with her.

He went to her flat. He stayed with her. All night.

Jealousy bit deep, like an animal attacking her, claws and teeth sunk into her flesh. She bent double in agony, her mind flashing with images of them together—Ben naked in Helen's bed, touching her, moving on her.

Oh, God! she thought. How can I bear it?

CHAPTER EIGHT

BEN'S key sounded in the lock, then she heard the click of high heels on the hall floor and Helen Manners saying, 'I've always loved this house, you know, Ben.'

Nerissa's teeth met. Well, you aren't getting it! she thought, angry blood rushing to her face. Or him, either! If Ben thinks he can divorce me and marry you that easily, he can forget it. Aunt Grace is right—I'm going to fight for him; I'm not just letting him go.

'It's spacious and comfortable, a perfect house for a family home,' agreed Ben.

'There's so much one could do with it,' Helen said. 'I'd love the chance to transform it. I can just see what it would look like if a good interior designer worked on it.'

They were right outside the door of the sitting-room now, their voices very clear. 'Thanks for last night, Helen,' Ben murmured. 'I was lucky I had you to turn to; I'm very grateful.'

Nerissa drew a harsh breath. God. She had been right; he had spent the night with Helen. The pain intensified and she screwed up her hands, biting down on her lip to stop herself groaning aloud. Any minute now they might walk in here, see her; she had to get control of herself, hide what was happening inside her. She mustn't let them see how much she minded.

'I won't forget it, Helen,' Ben said and Helen gave a husky little laugh.

'Neither will I.'

Damn her! thought Nerissa, her eyes blazing with jealous rage. It was bad enough to know what had happened—agonising to hear them talking to each other in this intimate, teasing way.

Ben laughed too. 'You're not going to hit me for a rise, are you?'

Nerissa drew an incredulous breath.

'I might, at that!' Helen said, her voice amused, light. 'How about that cup of tea you promised me, for a start?'

'I'll put the kettle on,' said Ben, and they walked on past, went into the kitchen.

Nerissa waited until she heard the door close on them, then she went upstairs to her bedroom, moving softly, carefully, avoiding a stair she knew creaked. She didn't want them to know she was in the house. She couldn't face a confrontation with them both; she didn't want to look into Helen Manners' face and see triumph, mockery, satisfaction there. It would damage her pride too much.

Part of her wanted to collect her case and walk out of the house again, go back to Lantern Farm, to people who loved her and whom she loved. Another part of her urged her to stay and fight, but she didn't know if she had the strength.

She lay down on her bed and stared at the ceiling, her mind a battleground. The house was silent again. They were still in the kitchen. Drinking tea— it sounded so homely and domesticated, so English and polite.

Except that adultery wasn't polite or homely. It was a destruction of the home; it ripped apart the fabric of a marriage.

Ben had said something like that, she suddenly remembered. He had bitterly accused her of committing adultery in her heart, with Philip. She couldn't deny it, either. There had been three in her bed ever since her wedding-day.

If only she could have those months back, start again, make her marriage real for the first time! Oh, why hadn't she discovered she loved Ben sooner? If only...

The two most bitter words in the English language, she thought grimly—if only... It was impossible to call back time, change the past. It was irrevocable; nobody could alter a blink of time.

The only thing you could do was deal with the consequences of the past, and at this moment that meant Ben having spent the night with Helen.

Had Ben discovered that he was in love with Helen?

She winced at that idea. If he had...she would have to let him go; she couldn't try to hold him if he loved someone else. However much it hurt, she would have to let him go.

But had they sounded like people in love? She frowned, thinking back over what she had overheard. Surely there hadn't been enough emotion in their voices? Amusement, mutual liking, intimacy...she had heard all that, but she had not heard love.

Oh, but what does love sound like? she angrily asked herself, and had no rational answer. It was all a matter of intuition. She had often suspected that Helen wanted Ben, but just now she hadn't heard deep emotion in Ben's voice.

And if he doesn't love her I'm not letting him go, thought Nerissa. I won't let her snatch him away from me—I'll fight her any way I can. I don't believe she'll make him happy. I believe I can.

Her heart gave a leap like a salmon fighting its way upstream against the current.

She looked into a future which shimmered with happiness. If only she could get Ben back ...

Now that I know I love him our marriage is going to be different, she thought. It had always been passionate—in fact, sex had been everything in their marriage and that had increasingly bothered her. Good sex wasn't enough. A woman needed more than that. The emptiness of their relationship had made her edgy, uneasy, troubled. All that had changed suddenly the moment when she realised she was in love with Ben.

Why couldn't she have worked it out just a day earlier? Ben wouldn't have left her, he wouldn't have gone to Helen and she wouldn't be lying here in utter misery while he was downstairs with another woman.

Oh, God, what if they came up here? Into this room to make love, go to bed together?

She jackknifed up to a sitting position, her knees against her chest, her head on top of them, rocking backwards and forwards, groaning softly.

Ben wouldn't. Not here. Not in their bedroom, in the bed they had shared together since their wedding-day.

Her face was white then crimson, a lily then a red rose. Her blue eyes were shadowed and haunted with visions. Pictures she wished she could stop seeing. If only you could turn your mind off like a television! She had never realised what a vivid imagination she had.

She knew all the ways Ben made love; she knew what he looked like, sounded like in the throes of desire. The very idea of him with another woman made her sick.

A sound downstairs made her freeze, listening intently. Their voices, in the hall again, drifted up the stairs. She swung her legs off the bed, turned to stare at the door, her ears beating with hypertension.

The noise of a slam made her jump, her nerves on edge. For a second she didn't realise what it was, then it dawned on her. That had been the front door closing.

They were leaving. She heard footsteps, the sound a car starting, driving away. Downstairs silence descended once more. The house lay around her, empty, cold, haunted.

She ran to the window to stare out, saw the car vanishing round the corner of the street.

For a second she was even relieved. Thank God they weren't coming up here; she wouldn't have to face them.

Then it dawned on her that Ben had left with Helen and the questions began buzzing in her head like wasps, stinging, driving her mad. Where were they going? Would he be coming back? What if he moved in with Helen, started living with her?

It was so easy to get a divorce these days—you separated for two years and, so long as it was agreed between the two partners, the court awarded you a divorce without further ado.

She would probably be awarded the matrimonial home—although as they had no children they might have to sell it and divide the proceeds. She wasn't sure about the legal niceties of divorce but Ben was a lawyer, he would know all the details and probabilities—especially as he had already been divorced.

She frowned, remembering his cutting remarks about Aileen's having demanded the house, the car, a large sum of money. Because of her adultery Ben had managed to counter-sue her, but he had still been forced to sell the home they had shared and give her half the money raised. His first marriage had made Ben very bitter and cynical.

I'm still paying Aileen's bill, thought Nerissa bleakly.

Well, she didn't want anything from him, not money, not this house. She didn't want to go on living in the home they had shared together; it would be too bitter.

Her frown deepened. Maybe Ben felt that way too? He might prefer to buy a new place, one which was free of memories of her.

That hurt too. Everything in her life since she became an adult had given her pain, she thought bitterly. She had fallen in love twice, and each time it had caused her anguish. She never wanted to fall in love again—never, never. She had been cured of love. You would have to be crazy to want to feel like this a third time!

She threw herself on the bed, face down, trying to shut out the light, wishing the house would fall on her and bury her forever, shuddering with sobs that wrenched her whole body.

Her crying was just beginning to slow down when a sound behind her made her jump, stiffen, lift her head. Her black hair was all over her white, tear-stained face and she peered through it like a wild animal in a thicket of thorns.

Ben stood by the bed, staring, his face blank with surprise. 'I thought I heard somebody up here...I thought you were a burglar.' He tossed aside the golf club he was holding in one hand; it fell across a chair and she watched without really thinking about it. 'I came prepared,' he told her, then said abruptly, 'You've been crying. He isn't worse, is he?'

'He?' she repeated, then realised he meant Philip and shook her head. 'No.'

'Then why the tears?' he asked in that curt, hard voice. 'Missing him already?'

She winced and he made an impatient sound.

'Oh, forget it,' he said. 'How long have you been here?'

'I got home an hour ago. You didn't leave with Helen?' Why had Helen left without him? Taken his car?

Ben didn't bother to answer the rhetorical question. 'You were up here all the time?' he thought aloud, frowning, no doubt wondering what she had heard, what she had guessed.

'Is she coming back?' Nerissa didn't bother to enlighten him—let him work it out for himself. 'I suppose she must be as she took your car.'

'Not my car,' he said impatiently. 'That was her car; she drove me back here.'

'It looked like your car!'

'She has the same model.'

'The same colour too,' Nerissa said sarcastically. 'Isn't that interesting? I wonder why she bought a car that's identical to yours?'

'How do I know? She liked my car, I suppose!'

Nerissa gave him a dry look. 'Or its owner? So, where is your car? At her flat?' The jealousy broke out; she couldn't keep up the calm façade. 'Don't lie to me, Ben! I'm not stupid—I realise you spent the night with her!'

He stiffened. 'What?'

He was playing for time, stalling; she knew that wary look in his face. Clever Ben, quick, shrewd, careful Ben—he had learnt every trick in the book during his legal training: when to stay silent, when to let a witness trip himself up, when to pounce and tear someone into shreds. Oh, he needn't think he fooled her. She knew him too well for that.

Angrily flushed, she sat up, eyed him with contempt. 'Is it the first time? Or has she been your mistress all along? Even before I met you? I always guessed she fancied you but it never occurred to me that you might be sleeping with her.'

His eyes narrowed, hardened into a glittering darkness. 'It wouldn't have bothered you if I had, though, would it? You don't give a damn what I do, or with whom! Why have you come back? To stop me naming your brother in my divorce suit? Did you tell them that I'd threatened that? Did they send you hurrying after me, to make sure I didn't do it? That's the only thing that bothers you, isn't it, Nerissa? The threat of scandal, of your precious family secret being exposed at last!'

'Don't try to change the subject! This has nothing to do with Philip, and anyway you know perfectly well you couldn't name Philip in a divorce—I've never been unfaithful to you since our wedding-day!'

'Physically!' he sneered.

'The law doesn't recognise emotions!' she threw back. 'You've told me that often enough. It doesn't matter, under the law, what you feel or think, only what you actually do. The guilty party in this divorce would be you, Ben.' Her jealousy made her voice rough, bitter. 'You slept with her. I never slept with Philip.'

'That's why you're still obsessed with him!' Ben's mouth twisted. 'All that frustrated passion feeds the obsession, won't let it die.' He caught her shoulders and shook her. 'Wake up, Nerissa! Before it's too late, wake up and realise what you're doing to your life, the waste of your emotions, of your capacity for loving... It makes me want to kill you sometimes.'

She believed him. He was handling her as if he might kill her any minute.

'You're hurting me!' she protested and he bared his teeth in a snarl, his features animal, primitive.

'Good. Damn you, I want to hurt you! I'd do anything to wake you up. You've been sleep-walking for too long. It's time you started living in the real world.'

'Is that why you spent the night with your secretary?' she threw at him. 'To hurt me?'

'Did it?' he asked, his voice curiously husky, and her angry colour all drained away. She looked up at him with wide, stricken blue eyes, trembling.

'What do you want, Ben? Blood?'

'Just the truth,' he said through grim lips which barely parted to let the words out.

'First tell me if you did sleep with her,' she said, turning the knife on her own pain. She had to know, however much it hurt. She couldn't bear this nagging suspicion, uncertainty, dread.

He shook his head, his mouth wry. 'No, Nerissa. I didn't sleep with Helen. I never have, never wanted to. She's a good secretary—I rely on her to run my working life—but that's all she has ever been to me.'

She drew a shaky breath, weak with relief—but could she believe him? 'Then where were you all night? I know you weren't here. Nobody slept here last night; that's obvious. The house is too tidy. You spent the night with Helen, in her flat. I heard you tell her how grateful you were.'

'I am grateful to her, but I didn't spend the night at her flat. I spent the night in a motel on the motorway. I ran into fog last night, but I wasn't in a mood to be sensible and slow down. In fact, I drove like a maniac and almost went straight into the back of a slow-moving lorry.'

She gasped, eyes widening. 'Ben! Oh, how could you be so stupid? You might have been killed!'

'I wasn't, though,' he said. 'I saw it at the last moment and swerved out of its way, on to the hard shoulder. I was going so fast I couldn't stop. The car ran up the bank and came down again with an almighty smash.'

'Were you hurt?' Nerissa went cold; her eyes flickered hurriedly over him looking for signs of injury, and he grimaced.

'No, I was damn lucky. If I hadn't been wearing my seatbelt I'd have gone through the windscreen and been killed. As it was, I ended up being thrown sideways, against the door. I got a bruised shoulderbone, cracked a couple of ribs. I feel as if I ache all over, and I had a headache all night, but otherwise I'm OK.'

She sighed in relief. It would have been her fault if he had been killed, or even, like Philip, seriously injured. She had suspected from the minute she'd heard about Philip's accident that she was, if only obliquely, to blame. Philip had been driving wildly because he was unhappy. Now Ben... I'm a jinx, she thought. I'm bad luck to the men I get involved with.

'The car came off badly, though,' Ben said. 'The bonnet crumpled like paper; the radiator cracked and water flooded out everywhere—boiling-hot water, too. I had to jump out of the way to avoid being scalded. Another car stopped and a very nice guy helped me get out of the car and drove me to the nearest phone to call out the AA to tow the car away. They also gave me a lift to the nearest motel.'

'Where does Helen come into this, though?' Nerissa asked uncertainly.

'I rang Helen to tell her where I was in case she needed to get in touch with me. She offered to come and get me, drive me back. I could have hired a car, but Helen insisted on coming.'

'I bet she did!' muttered Nerissa, and Ben's eyes narrowed on her, gleaming and quick. She flushed at that look and hurriedly asked, 'So she drove up to this motel, last night? And she stayed there too?'

Drily, he said, 'She thought I might have delayed shock and it might not be wise to drive myself back, and she could be right. I was grateful not to have to drive again so soon. And if she had waited until this morning to drive up there, we wouldn't have got back until this evening, and it was essential that I get back to London before midday. Helen had been trying to get in touch with me to tell me that she had made a lunch appointment for me with one of the Euro MPs to discuss a case he wants me to take up.'

'That's where you've been this morning? Having lunch with this politician?'

He nodded. 'It's an important case and it could be worth a lot of money to the practice. Helen knew I'd want it, and the client was only going to be in London today—he's off to Brussels tonight and won't be back for some weeks. It was important that I see him so she made the appointment, guessing I'd be free as I had no official engagements. She thought I'd get there somehow, but then she couldn't get in touch with me. She wasn't getting any answer from the farm, so she kept leaving me messages on our answerphone.'

'I know; I heard them when I played back the tape.' Nerissa watched him, wondering if he knew how Helen felt about him. Ben might say Helen was just his secretary and he had never been interested in her as anything else, but Nerissa was convinced that Helen had very different feelings about him. Didn't he know that?

'Helen's a first-class secretary,' Ben said drily.

'And in love with you!'

'There's nothing between us, Nerissa. If you're hoping to be able to use Helen against me in a divorce, forget it. I've never so much as kissed the woman.'

She was silent, believing him.

He waited, then said, 'Did you follow me back to London to protect your brother and your family reputation? Don't tell me what you think I want to hear, Nerissa—tell me the truth; that's all I want.'

'I've never lied to you!'

His black brows arched sardonically. 'No?'

'No, Ben. I told you the truth about . . . about me and Philip . . . before I agreed to marry you. I didn't lie.'

'Sometimes I wish to God you had!' Ben said bitterly, then closed his eyes, groaned aloud. 'No, strike that! It wouldn't have made it any easier not to know. I had to know the truth. If I had found out later I think it might have destroyed me.'

With his eyes shut he looked like a carved stone statue—stark, spare features, reined mouth, clenched jaw, and those hooded, blind eyes. She could stare at him without Ben's seeing her expression, in no danger of his glimpsing the need and hunger in her face.

Her eyes moved, flickering passionately; she ached to touch him, to pull him down on to the bed with her—perhaps that was the way to reach him now? It had always worked in the past for them. Their bodies had met in the dark in this room night after night, and while they made passionate love they forgot all their other differences, everything outside this room, this house.

His lids lifted suddenly and she found herself looking into those deep, dark-pupilled eyes. His stare was so intense it was like being sucked into a black hole in space. She trembled feverishly, her mouth dry. It was as if... almost as if... Ben had picked up what she was thinking just now. That had happened before. He was always reading her mind, especially in moments like this, when her senses were dominating her and she wasn't thinking so much as feeling.

'We always had one way of communicating, didn't we?' he murmured and her heart began crashing into her ribs.

His hands tightened on her shoulders, drew her toward him, his face taut, darkly flushed.

'No, Ben!' she said, struggling; she couldn't bear to let him make love to her when he didn't love her. Not any more, never again.

Until now it hadn't mattered; she had let the craving of her body dictate what she did but she hadn't known she loved him, then. She knew now. 'I can't,' she cried out.

His grey eyes flared, smoky as dark fires. He pushed her backwards, pinned her shoulders down on the bed, leaned over her, his face brooding, dangerous.

'I told you at the farm before I left, Nerissa— from now on this marriage has got to be a real one. No more compromises, no more pretences. Either go or stay—but if you stay I want him out of your head, out of your heart.'

'It isn't that easy,' she began and his lip curled in a snarl.

'I don't care if it's easy or not. Those are the only terms I'm offering.'

'He's my brother, Ben! I can't push him, or my father, or Aunt Grace, out of my life. It took a long time for me to come to terms with the truth. It was such a shock, in the beginning, I couldn't take it in—but I finally did, while I was up there this time. I'll always be fond of him, and remember our childhood as a very happy time, but I'm not in love with him. I don't even know if I ever was. It was just that there was nobody else—I never went anywhere, knew very few people, and Philip was always there, and we got on so well...it seemed natural...' She stopped, wincing at the word she had used. 'How were we to know it was the very opposite? Until they told us. But it is over now, for both of us.'

Ben's eyes were grim, searching. 'That wasn't the impression I got when I saw you together in that hospital ward.'

She sighed, trying to convince him, make him understand. 'That was such a charged moment! I was so relieved that he was going to be OK. Yet in a funny kind of way I think that was when I began to realise——' She broke off, flushed and breathless, and Ben's eyes fixed on her intently.

'Realise what?'

She sought helplessly for words that wouldn't betray her. She couldn't bear him to know she was in love with him. Her pride had taken enough of a battering already.

'That...I'd changed...' She avoided meeting his eyes, desperate to hide her feelings.

She heard Ben's intake of air. Huskily, he said, 'Look at me, Nerissa!'

She flickered a glance upwards, and the way he was looking at her made her pulses go wild.

'I'm not imagining it, am I?' he whispered.

'What?' she breathed through lips that quivered.

He lowered his head and she felt him breathing against her throat, his warm lips brushing her skin, the scent of him in her nostrils, tactile sensations that made every nerve in her body beat with reaction.

'That you aren't quite as indifferent to me as you used to be,' he said in a voice that wasn't quite steady.

'I was never indifferent...'

'Not in bed,' he agreed, and his hand moved in a slow caress, following the curved contours of her body which immediately responded with trembling excitement, perspiration breaking out on her skin, her blood running faster.

Her breath caught but she groaned, 'Don't, Ben, not unless——' She stopped, unable to finish that sentence, to admit what she wanted, what she needed from him.

'Unless what?' he murmured into her throat, his lips sliding downwards, pushing aside her collar, exploring the smooth valley between her breasts where her heart beat so hard, she knew he must be able to hear it.

She had to stop him. She couldn't let him make love to her ever again, unless there was more to it than desire, a need for pleasure. She pushed his head away, and even then her skin shivered at the feel of his hair against her palm.

'I don't want to go on with our marriage,' she said fiercely.

He froze, his head back, the stab of his grey eyes piercing her to the heart. That was how Ben looked when he was at his angriest—icy, remote, yet behind that was a rage that was hotter than hell.

'So you are choosing him?' he bit out between tight teeth.

'No! This has nothing to do with Philip.' His mouth writhed in a sneer and she cried out, 'Don't look at me like that! I'm telling you the truth. Philip's my brother, nothing else now. This is about you and me.'

He stiffened, watching her, his face pale now.

Gently she said, 'Ben, try to understand . . . sex just isn't enough. Oh, in the beginning I thought it would be; I found you very attractive and I enjoyed making love to you. In fact, for a long time, sex was like a drug, helping me to bear the pain of losing Philip—when we made love it drove everything else out of my head. I didn't care what happened to me, you see; I didn't believe I would ever fall in love again.'

'And now you think you could?' Ben said slowly. 'You want me to set you free, so that you can start looking for someone else?'

Nerissa didn't know how to answer. She was sick of lies and half-truths, of pretences and disguises. If Ben didn't love her, if all he wanted from her was her body, she couldn't stay with him. It would be a living hell.

'Is that what you want?' Ben repeated in a terse, furious voice, and his anger made her even more nervous.

She really couldn't bear any more of this.

'Yes,' she whispered.

CHAPTER NINE

FOR a second Ben didn't react. Nerissa didn't know what he was thinking. His face was his court face—blank, icy, remote.

What was he thinking? Did he care if she left him or not? Oh, God, she thought, he'll walk away and not look back. I shouldn't have followed him to London. I'm going to lose him.

It was the second time this had happened to her now—these unexpected blows of fate leaving her no choice but to go away, alone.

Why does it keep happening to me? she thought. If it's a pattern, who sets it up? Not me. I hardly pick the same type; this isn't a rerun of the same situation. They couldn't be more different—Ben and Philip have nothing in common, except that I fell in love with them. Yet here I am again, watching fate snatching away my chance of happiness. Why?

Then she heard Ben make a deep, harsh sound in his throat. She looked back at him. He had turned a dark, angry red. His eyes glittered. The very air seemed to pulse visibly with danger.

Nerissa felt like someone standing on the lip of a volcano, watching the heat and lava within.

The volcano exploded suddenly, in a roar that made her jump. 'I'm damned if I will!'

Her blue eyes widened in shock. Her hair stood up on the nape of her neck, even her scalp prickling, as if she had just grabbed hold of a live electric cable.

'You really think I'd shrug and let you go, stand back and watch you dating other men, falling in love with someone else——?' He stopped, swallowing, his throat moving visibly, convulsively, as if it hurt him.

Shakily, Nerissa whispered, 'You said you wanted a divorce! When you left the farm, you said you——'

'I know what I said!' he interrupted harshly, his eyes dark and brooding. 'That's what you've reduced me to—making empty threats to try to force you to stay with me! Can you have any idea what that does to my pride? Having to choose between making stupid threats or begging on my knees?'

Her heart turned over and she began to shake, staring at him, trying to read those glittering grey eyes. 'Ben...'

He scowled at her. 'Well, now you know!' he muttered.

She couldn't believe what she was seeing in his face, hearing in his voice.

'Are you saying...? Ben, do you...? What are you saying...?' she stammered, going white with tension, with painful hope, with fear that she could be imagining this because it was what she desperately wanted.

He stared at her fixedly, suddenly said, 'Oh, to hell with pride! Look what it has done to your family!' He paused, drew a long, rough breath then said hoarsely, 'I'm crazy about you, OK?'

She could scarcely breathe.

Ben looked at her and away, his lids down over his restless eyes. 'If you laugh, I'll kill you.'

'I wouldn't...Ben, I wouldn't dream of it...' she protested.

'No, of course you wouldn't,' he said flatly. 'You aren't like Aileen. She enjoyed humbling my pride, making me squirm. After what she did to me, I swore I'd never put myself in a woman's power again. I wasn't letting myself get hurt that way twice.'

'I never wanted to hurt you, Ben!' she whispered, and he sighed.

'I believe you, but you know the old saying...the road to hell is paved with good intentions!'

She laughed huskily.

He watched her, his eyes wry. 'You're such a feminine creature, Nerissa. You're my opposite in many ways. You're gentle, for a start, but my clients pay me to be tough and tenacious when I'm fighting for them. I have to have a mind like a razor, but you're dreamy and romantic. Maybe I value your female qualities just because they're what I lack.' His mouth twisted cynically. 'But that wasn't what made me fall in love with you. I can't pretend it was your mind or your heart I fell for—it was that beautiful body of yours.'

The heat of his eyes made her skin hot too; she looked down, trembling violently.

'From the first second I saw you, at that party,' he said thickly, 'I took one look and wanted you. I loved the way you moved, your mouth, your big blue eyes, all that black hair, and that wistful look... You turned me on at first sight. After my divorce, I was in no mood to get serious about any woman—I had made up my mind not to marry again, but you were totally different from Aileen, in every possible way. She was as hard as nails, but you looked as if you needed to be taken care of— and I wanted to do just that. Everything I saw, I liked—then I took another look and realised it hadn't hit you like that. It was obvious you simply weren't interested.'

She couldn't deny it; she hadn't been interested in anything at all at the time. She had noticed him, though, or rather he had made enough of an impression for her to remember him when he'd rung her later.

He grimaced, mocking himself. 'I thought at first you were just playing hard to get and I set out to be charming, to chat you up and make an impression—but I didn't, did I? You simply didn't see me! And I couldn't make you take notice of me, either. So I told myself to walk away, forget about you, but I couldn't do it. In the end I rang and asked you out. I was scared stiff you would turn me down flat.'

'I almost did,' she remembered, sighing. She had had no idea that Ben was seriously attracted to her—she had never thought about him again after that first meeting until he'd rung her to ask for a date, and then she had hesitated about accepting.

Ben laughed shortly. 'I knew it. Even at the time. I despised myself for pursuing you when it was clear you couldn't care less, but I had to see you again. I even told myself that, once I had, I'd be able to forget you, but seeing you again only made it worse. Once wasn't enough. I had to go on seeing you. It began to be what I lived for...'

Nerissa was stunned, staring at him, not believing her ears.

Ben watched her expression, grimaced at it. 'And
you had no idea, did you?'

She dumbly shook her head.

'No, it was clear you had no notion what you
were doing to me,' he said with bitterness. 'Aileen
had given my pride quite a battering, but it was as
nothing compared to what you did to me.'

'Ben, I didn't even guess...' she broke out and
he groaned.

'That's the whole point. You were on my mind
all the time, nagging away at me, like a thorn under
the skin. I couldn't get rid of you. I wasn't sleeping
well, couldn't concentrate, couldn't think. I knew
by then that I was in the grip of an obsession, an
infatuation—well, that's what I told myself. I preferred to think of it that way. I wasn't admitting I
had fallen in love with you—my pride wouldn't let
me use that word. But, whatever I called it, you
had exploded in my life like an earthquake—on the
Richter scale, you had hit me with a shattering
eight—about as high as it's possible to go! But I
could see that I wasn't even making your needle go
as high as one.'

'I was in the grip of an obsession of my own,'
Nerissa said, then looked at him uneasily, afraid
that he would get angry again.

'I soon knew that,' he said, his mouth hard.
'There was nobody else around you in London, so
I deduced that it had to be someone from your past.
I thought maybe he was a married man and you
had left home to break with him. That was why I
insisted on visiting your home. When we got to the

farm, I knew at once that it was Philip. At first I couldn't understand why the two of you had broken up—there seemed no reason why you should have parted. There was no mention of a quarrel, and seeing you together made it crystal-clear that you both felt the same way.'

Sadly, she said, 'We were both trying so hard, though. We hardly said a word to each other, barely looked at each other!'

'Very obviously,' Ben drily said. 'You tried *too* hard. Every now and then you would snatch a quick look at him, or he would walk past and you would both suddenly stop talking—and his parents were so edgy. I could have cut the atmosphere with a knife. I wondered if his parents objected to a marriage on the grounds that you were first cousins, and that was when I realised how alike you were— there was such a strong family resemblance. Almost as if you were twins, I thought, and suddenly I had a flash of intuition... Could you actually be brother and sister? It would explain everything, but it seemed incredible to think what I was thinking. I couldn't believe it at first, but I kept noticing the odd looks, the broken sentences, the tension every time you were both in the same room, and the more I watched the two of you, the more I felt sure I was right.'

'I suppose you developed your intuition over years of working in court,' Nerissa said.

'Years of second-guessing the criminal classes!' he agreed, his mouth crooked with amusement.

'You're very clever, anyway. None of our neigh- bours ever guessed. Oh, they saw that I was very

like Philip, but they just put it down to our being
cousins.'

'They'd known you all your lives, they were used
to thinking of you as cousins, and they only knew
you from the outside, from seeing you around the
village. They weren't there, in that house, picking
up the vibes between all of you.'

'I'm amazed you married me, knowing about
him, Ben.'

'You forget what an arrogant bastard I am! I
wanted you so much I'd have done anything to get
you, and once I knew about him I told myself it
would be easy to make you forget him.'

'If you had told me you loved me——'

'You'd have run a mile!' he said, his face sardonic. 'I had trouble enough convincing you that
marriage would work for us when all we had in
common was a physical attraction. And anyway,
my pride would never have let me admit how I felt
when I knew you didn't feel the same.'

'Oh, pride again...' Nerissa shivered. 'It causes
nothing but disaster!'

Ben nodded. 'It was Aileen's legacy, in my case.
She had taught me to protect myself from getting
hurt again. I thought I could marry you and wait
for you to turn to me. I hadn't bargained for the
way it would feel to have an invisible rival between
us day and night. Every time I made love to you I
felt you were thinking about him. I'd lie beside you
in bed, wide awake all night, knowing you were
probably dreaming about him, not me. It was
unbearable.'

Softly, she said, 'To love and not be loved
in return?'

Ben looked into her eyes, his face whitening, turning as pale as death. He hated admitting it, she recognised, and put her hand up, caressed his cheek tenderly.

'I know all about that. I've been so miserable, Ben, since yesterday, when you walked out on me.'

His breath caught. He was very still, watching her.

'I don't know when I started loving you,' she said. 'A long time ago, I think. But it only dawned on me when I thought I'd lost you forever.'

Ben took a long, rough breath but didn't say anything, just watched her with fierce eyes.

'I love you,' she said, clasping his face between both hands and looking into his eyes, allowing all her feelings to show in her face.

'I wish to God I was sure...' Ben muttered, a little tic jerking beside his mouth.

She stared at his parted lips, traced the passionate outline of them with one finger, saw his eyes half close, his nostrils flare, heard the intake of his breath.

'Ben...how often do you want me to say it? I love you,' she whispered.

'What about him?'

The grate of the question told her how jealous Ben had been, still was, and she sighed.

'I told you...it's over. It has been for a long time, Ben. I would never have wanted you so badly if I had been in love with someone else. I should have known that, right at the beginning, but I was confused. I knew I wanted you but I thought I loved Philip. How could I love two men? So I told myself it was just chemistry between you and me—a physical attraction, it didn't mean a thing. After all, you told me that was how you felt!'

He groaned. 'So if I hadn't lied I wouldn't have had to go through a hell of jealousy?' Then he frowned, shook his head. 'No, Nerissa, it would have scared you rigid if I'd told you how I felt at the beginning. The last thing you wanted then was any emotional demands.'

'Maybe you're right,' she said uncertainly. 'It took a long time for me to realise I loved you...'

Ben's eyes darkened with feeling. 'Nerissa... Oh, God, Nerissa... I seem to have waited all my life to hear you say that.'

He kissed her fiercely, groaning, and she kissed him back, pierced with an answering desire, her body arching and trembling in wild excitement as she met his lips, her arms going round his neck, moving against him restlessly.

Ben laughed huskily in his throat. 'Are you in a hurry, darling?'

'Yes,' she said feverishly, twining around him, pulling him down on her. 'Make love to me, Ben. Make love to me.'

A year later, Nerissa gave birth to a son whom she and Ben called John, after her father. He was a large, healthy child with a thick mop of black hair, a clear, pale skin, a good pair of lungs which he used vigorously and quick, intelligent eyes like his father's.

'He's just like you!' Nerissa said to Ben.

'No, he's like you,' Ben said.

He was like both of them, of course, and they thought him remarkable, the most amazing baby ever born.

'Look at his little pink feet,' Nerissa said, stroking them. 'Look at his ears, Ben; aren't they perfect?'

He was a source of permanent wonder to her; she could watch him for hours, and so could Ben, although he tried to be impartial and said several times, 'He is just a baby, like all the others in the nursery, darling!'

'None of them is as perfect as Johnny!' she indignantly told him and Ben laughed.

'Well, maybe not.'

He was teasing her and she knew it, even though she pretended to be cross with him. It was all part of their new intimacy—the ability to laugh at each other, tease each other; they were all easy together now. The intense need hadn't altered but there had been a shift in the balance of their relationship. They fitted together as if they were Siamese twins, and it made both of them very happy.

Grace and John Thornton travelled down from the farm a fortnight after the baby arrived, to see it for the first time. At the last minute they rang to say they were bringing Philip with them. Nerissa was back home by then, although she had had the baby in the local maternity hospital. She had not had an easy birth—she was too slender, her hips too narrow and she was still recovering from the long ordeal. She had been ordered by her doctor to take it slowly for a while, so she was in bed, but sitting up, her black hair brushed and gleaming around her flushed face, wearing a lacy jacket over

a pink silk nightdress, her baby in a swinging cradle
beside the bed.

It was early autumn—mellow and golden. The
house had been tranquil and quiet all morning and
she had lain peacefully listening to it with con-
tented eyes. Suddenly it was full of voices and
movement. She heard them coming up the stairs,
heard Ben's deep, assured voice, smiled to herself.

He was happy. So was she, and even happier because she knew she was making Ben happy. The
new baby completed their marriage, turned them
into a family, not diminishing their love for each
other, but if anything increasing it, giving it a new
dimension.

His presence in the house was changing that, too.
It had been an elegant, gracious, peaceful house,
with antiques displayed on highly polished furniture and silk and brocade everywhere.

Now it was a family home. There were baby
clothes drying on the washing-line outside on the
terrace in the sunshine, and one room had been
made into a nursery—pastel-painted, with nursery-
rhyme wallpaper, a row of soft toys on a shelf and
a baby bath, nappies, zinc cream, talc, bath oil,
and all the other impedimenta of a baby's life. For
something so small he took up an awful lot of room,
and he made a great deal of noise at times—especially at night.

Nerissa worried about that. Ben liked the house
to be quiet while he was working at legal documents, reading case law, studying a client's depo-
sition. Every time the baby began to yell Nerissa
snatched him up, but then, remembering what her
aunt had told her about a husband sometimes

feeling left out when a baby arrived, she started fretting in case Ben should feel shut out, start resenting baby Johnny.

Especially as they hadn't made love for weeks! The last phase of her pregnancy had been troubled, the doctor had advised them not to make love, and now it would be some time before they could start sleeping together again.

So she had gone to some trouble to make sure that Ben did not feel that the whole house now revolved around their child. Although she had him by her bed most of the day, Nerissa put the baby into his own room in the evenings, and especially at night.

They might not be able to make love yet, but Ben could lie on the bed beside her when he came home from work. They could kiss and cuddle, Ben could tell her about his day in court, groan about being overworked, complain about his clients, and Nerissa could talk about her own day.

As soon as she was pregnant it had started—she had discovered a whole new universe of women. Her guides had been the wives of Ben's colleagues, most particularly those with small children, who were pleased to add her to their daily routine of baby clinic, shopping, help, gossip and advice over the tables in the nearby coffee shop or in each other's homes. Some of them had wheedled her into babysitting for them on the theory that the sooner she got her hand in the better!

She had given up her job halfway through her pregnancy. The constant travelling involved in working for the office design firm had made it impossible—especially as hers had not been an easy

pregnancy. She had had ghastly morning sickness
for weeks, and then had often felt faint if she had
to bend down or walk too far. She had been advised to rest a good deal during the last stage of
her pregnancy anyway, and as she had decided to
look after the baby herself there seemed no point
in getting a new job, although she might go back
to work with some other firm later—unless she had
another child.

She was excited by the arrival of her family. It
seemed an age since she had last seen them. She
had talked to Aunt Grace on the phone throughout
her pregnancy, had written home with her news,
and Aunt Grace had written back with her own,
telling her that Philip was home, was getting better
all the time, and then was working again, was just
fine; that Uncle John was well, the farm was in
good shape.

Aunt Grace and Uncle John had come to London
to stay with her and Ben in the spring, and again
in the summer, but she had not seen Philip, who
had stayed at home to look after the farm.

Nerissa was eager to see their reaction to this first
sight of her baby. She knew Aunt Grace was going
to love him.

In fact, Aunt Grace was the first into the room,
smiling, bustling over to the bed to hug her.

'Well, you look bonny, lass! Ben says you had a
bad time? You look fine now, though, and it was
worth it, wasn't it?' She glanced sideways at the
cradle, the occupant stirring at the sound of her
voice, setting his cradle swinging. 'And there he is…
Oh, the little lamb—he's got your eyes, blue as

cornflowers... He's wide awake, too, isn't he? Taking everything in! Can I pick him up?'

Nerissa nodded, smiling, and Aunt Grace lifted the baby out of the cradle with practised, capable hands.

'Well, look at you!' she cooed at him. 'My word, you're a big lad—big bones, like your father. You're going to be tall and broad-backed. You don't take after your mother that way.' She looked at her husband, who had kissed Nerissa. 'He's like you too, John. Can you see it? Look at these great big feet! I'd know those knobbly toes anywhere.'

He began laughing.

Nerissa looked past him at the door. Philip stood there, smiling at her. He looked so brown and well—his old self again. She broke into a delighted smile and felt Ben watching her intently. His jealousy might have begun to fade, but it wasn't actually a corpse yet. She slid him a quick, re-assuring glance, silently sending him the message that he needn't look like that—there was nothing left of her old passion for her half-brother.

'Doesn't Philip look well, Ben?' she asked, and Ben gave her a wry look, nodding.

'Fit as a fiddle.'

Nerissa turned her eyes to Philip again, just as someone else came up behind him. Someone her own age, a slim, shapely girl in a bright blue wool dress belted tightly at her small waist. Nerissa recognised that face with a start of incredulity.

'Staff Nurse Courtney?' What on earth was she doing here?

'Megan,' Philip said, and Nerissa looked back at him quickly, her eyes widening.

They had always been able to read each other's mind.

He gave her his slow, warm smile. 'We've seen a lot of each other since I came out of hospital, Megan and I. We got engaged two days ago—Mum was dying to tell you on the phone, but I thought we'd save the news until we could tell you ourselves.'

Nerissa went on looking at him, searching his face, aware of the others watching her, trying to read her own expression. All she cared about at that moment was Philip; would he be happy with Megan Courtney? Was he just marrying her on the rebound, because he was tired of being alone, or was it the real thing? Did he love Megan Courtney? her eyes asked and Philip's steady eyes answered, warm as firelight. Yes he was telling her, he loved Megan. She saw that it was not the sort of love she and Ben had for each other—no fever and fret, no urgent, driving need. But there was something as powerful—a contentment, a calm happiness— which shone out of both of them.

Nerissa gave a little sigh of relief.

She looked at Megan, smiling warmly, held out both hands. 'Welcome to the family, Megan—what wonderful news. I hope you and Philip are going to be very happy.'

'She fits in with us all; we've got very fond of her,' Aunt Grace said comfortably, patting Megan's arm. 'She and Philip will come and live at the farm, but Megan wants to go on working for a bit, not start a family right away. You and Ben and little John must come for Christmas—we can have a real family Christmas this year!'

'We'd love that, wouldn't we, Ben?' Nerissa said, sliding him another look, and he nodded.

'That sounds very pleasant.'

Aunt Grace handed the baby to Megan. 'Don't you think he looks like my husband, dear?'

'Very much,' Megan said. 'He's gorgeous, Nerissa. It's making me very broody to cuddle him. Don't babies smell simply wonderful?' She looked into the baby's blue eyes and cooed, 'Hello, Johnny, I'm your aunt Megan . . .'

Nerissa realised that Philip would have told Megan the truth about her birth; Philip wouldn't want any secrets between him and his wife. He had learnt, like her, that pride was a destructive force, that secrets could hurt.

She lay back against her pillows while the family gathered round her bed, talking, laughing, admiring the baby. Nerissa watched them all, looking from one to the other, her eyes lingering longest on Ben. She had never been so happy in her life.

It began to rain outside—a brief shower, with dark clouds passing overhead—but in this room there was nothing but sunshine.

Coming Next Month

HARLEQUIN ✦ PRESENTS®

#1821 UNWANTED WEDDING Penny Jordan
(Top Author)
Rosy had to be married within three months. Guard Jamieson was successful, sexy—and single. With no other candidate available to walk her down the aisle, it looked as if Rosy would have to accept Guard's offer to help her out.

#1822 DEADLY RIVALS Charlotte Lamb
(Book Two: SINS)
When Olivia first met Max she was utterly captivated. But Max was her father's business enemy and she was forbidden to see him again. Four years later she agreed to marry Christos, Max's nephew. Then Max returned to claim her....

#1823 TWO'S COMPANY Carole Mortimer
(9 TO 5)
Juliet's boss has left her half his company but she has to share it with Liam, his son, who is sure that she seduced his father. Nor does she want him to know that she was engaged to his despised younger brother. Will he find out her dark secret?

#1824 A SAVAGE BETRAYAL Lynne Graham
(This Time, Forever)
Mina and Cesare had met again, four years after he rejected her as a gold-digging tramp! Now he was determined to marry her, but only to pursue his revenge on Mina.

#1825 SPRING BRIDE Sandra Marton
(Landon's Legacy: Book 4)
Kyra's father's legacy would allow her to assert her independence. Antonio would help her—but at a price! He wanted to own her completely—and if she succumbed Kyra knew she would never be free again.

#1826 PERFECT CHANCE Amanda Carpenter
(Independence Day)
Mary's life was reasonably happy—until the day Chance Armstrong walked into it! He was offering her the perfect chance for a lot of excitement and the most exciting challenge of all.... He asked Mary to marry him!

Where there's a will there's a way...
for four charismatic characters to find love

by Sandra Marton
Book 4: #1825 SPRING BRIDE

When Charles Landon dies, he leaves behind a
different legacy for each of his children: for vulnerable
Kyra Landon this means a passionate encounter with
Antonio Rodrigo Cordoba del Rey—a man way
out of her league?

For Cade, Grant, Zach and Kyra, Landon's Legacy
is the key to their happiness—and very special love
matches that will last a lifetime!

Harlequin Presents: you'll want to know
what happens next!

Available in July wherever Harlequin books are sold.

HARLEQUIN PRESENTS®

If you are looking for more titles by

CHARLOTTE LAMB

Don't miss these fabulous stories by one of
Harlequin's great authors:

Harlequin Presents®

#11370	DARK PURSUIT	$2.75	☐
#11467	HEART ON FIRE	$2.89	☐
#11480	SHOTGUN WEDDING	$2.89	☐
#11560	SLEEPING PARTNERS	$2.99	☐
#11584	FORBIDDEN FRUIT	$2.99	☐
#11618	DREAMING	$2.99	☐
#11706	GUILTY LOVE	$2.99 U.S.	☐
		$3.50 CAN.	☐
#11720	VAMPIRE LOVER	$3.25 U.S.	☐
		$3.75 CAN.	☐

The following titles are part of the Barbary Wharf series

#11498	BESIEGED	$2.89	☐
#11509	BATTLE FOR POSSESSION	$2.89	☐
#11530	A SWEET ADDICTION	$2.89	☐

(limited quantities available on certain titles)

TOTAL AMOUNT	$
POSTAGE & HANDLING	$
($1.00 for one book, 50¢ for each additional)	
APPLICABLE TAXES*	$_____
TOTAL PAYABLE	$_____

(check or money order—please do not send cash)

To order, complete this form and send it, along with a check or money order
for the total above, payable to Harlequin Books, to: **In the U.S.:** 3010 Walden
Avenue, P.O. Box 9047, Buffalo, NY 14269-9047; **In Canada:** P.O. Box 613,
Fort Erie, Ontario, L2A 5X3.

Name: _____

Address: _____ City: _____

State/Prov.: _____ Zip/Postal Code: _____

*New York residents remit applicable sales taxes.
Canadian residents remit applicable GST and provincial taxes.   HCLBACK4

HARLEQUIN®